SIN BIN

TEAGAN HUNTER

SPECIAL EDITION COVER

Editing by Editing by C. Marie

Proofreading by Judy's Proofreading & Julia Griffis

Cover Design: Emily Wittig Designs

For the St. Louis Blues.
Sometimes you make me scream and yell.
Sometimes you make me cry.
But all of the time?
All of the time, you make me Bleed Blue.
Thank you for the memories.

CHAPTER 1

"Wicked Witch incoming in five minutes!"

I shake my head at the announcement that comes from my co-workers every morning.

Really, as a manager, I should discourage that kind of talk, but…it's true. Tori Witt, our media relations director, emulates Wicked Witch vibes. To say she's all business and no fun would be an understatement. Last year, when we crushed our social media number goals, she ordered six donuts and left out a sheet of gold stars next to them in the break room.

There are over ten employees on the social media staff alone. It was beyond insulting to all our hard work.

"I can't wait for the day when *you're* the director of the department," Blake, my co-worker, says, bumping his shoulder into mine.

"Me? Please. Like that will happen."

I mean, I'd *love* for it to happen, but I'm not holding my breath. They'd have to pry the job of director from Tori's cold, dead hands.

"I don't know…I heard a rumor…"

I roll my eyes. "People need to stop spreading rumors. Look what happened to Jane—she got fired because of rumors."

"Oh, no," Courtney says, handing me a piece of paper. "That one was true. We even have a new policy about it."

"Seriously?" I take the paper from Courtney's outstretched hand, mouth slackened.

She nods. "Yep. They even bolded it."

I glance at the sheet in my hand to see if it's true.

And it is. Right there in giant, bold print.

ROMANTIC RELATIONSHIPS WITH PLAYERS ARE PROHIBITED AND WILL RESULT IN IMMEDIATE TERMINATION.

"They dated, but he broke it off and she was upset. To get revenge, she tried to sue for sexual misconduct, saying the player came on to her, but he had a whole slew of texts that showed it was just the opposite. So now it's not just *discouraged*—it's prohibited." She shrugs. "So, much to everyone's chagrin because those guys are *hot*, no sleeping with the players."

I swallow back the lump that's formed in my throat.

Immediate termination.

"You don't have to worry about that from her," Blake

says. "She's on her way to director. There's no way she'll mess that shot up."

"What? You are? Does that mean the rumor about Tori is true? I—"

"Emilia! Blake! My office now!"

Tori's sharp words cut off whatever Courtney was going to say, and I glance over at Blake, whose brows are raised, just as shocked by Tori's interruption.

"Uh-oh," he says, setting his empty mug down. "Guess we're in trouble."

I press a hand over my stomach, trying to quell the nausea rolling through me as I look down at the paper in my hands because...*does she know?*

My face must show my worry because Blake laughs.

"I was teasing. Come on. We'll grab coffee afterward."

I give a polite laugh and follow him from the break room, spending the entire way there trying not to freak out over how serious Tori sounded when she blazed through the floor.

We slip into her office, close the door, and take the seats in front of her desk. She's sitting behind it looking every bit the director that she is. She's a small woman, a few inches shorter than me, but she can command a room like nobody's business. If I wasn't so terrified of her, I'd be in awe.

She stares at us down her nose, clacking her long nails against the top of her desk.

Clack.

Clack.

Clack.

Then finally, she speaks.

"I'm quitting."

I sit up straighter in my chair, leaning forward because maybe I didn't hear that correctly.

"You're quitting?" I ask, just to make sure, because there is no way she just said what I think she did.

Tori nods, her pin-straight, short dark bob bouncing. "Yes."

"Are you insane?" The words fly out of my mouth before I can stop them.

There's a sucked-in breath from next to me, and I can't say I blame Blake for his surprise.

I'm surprised.

Tori is a notorious hard-ass. In the two and a half years I've been working with the Comets, I'm certain I've only seen her smile twice, and once was when the team won the Stanley Cup, which doesn't really count. Smiles are contagious then.

Sitting here, watching her throwing her head back and laughing, is alarming. I won't lie and say I'm not shaking on the inside right now, waiting for her to explode on me.

"No, not insane," she says with a grin. "Just pregnant. So maybe a little insane, then, given my age."

My eyes widen because I had no idea Tori was expecting. I would have never guessed she even wanted children considering her disdain toward any event involving them.

"Is there something in the air?"

Again, my mouth betrays me, the words tumbling free without warning.

Blake bumps his knee against mine—*hard*.

Tori tips her head. "Pardon?"

I wave my hand. "Nothing. Just...a lot of babies happening around here is all."

"Ah." She purses her lips, nodding. "I assume you mean Mr. Lowell. We did send him and his...well, whatever she is to him, a card, yes?" She flicks her wrist, not caring if we sent something or not to the team's captain. She does it to save face, not because she truly cares about the players or their families.

I want to tell her Lowell's "whatever" has a name. It's Hollis, and she's been my best friend since first grade. But I'm sure with my insubordinate outbursts so far this morning, that likely wouldn't go over too well.

"Yes, we sent Mr. Lowell a congratulations card," Blake speaks up for me like the angel he is.

I am *so* buying him lunch today.

"Good." Tori folds her hands over her still flat stomach. "I won't be leaving until after the season ends, but you're my top picks for director. I wanted you both to know in advance because this second half of the season is going to be a test run of how well you'll handle this department in my absence. It will let me know if I can recommend one of you for the position without worrying about you ruining all my hard work, or if I need to look at outside sources to take over."

"A test run?"

Ugh. Why do I keep asking stupid questions?

And why does Tori *let* me keep asking stupid questions? Usually, she'd be reaming me a new one. Perhaps it's her pregnancy. Maybe she's turning a new kinder, gentler leaf.

"Yes, a test run. Nepotism may have gotten you this position, Emilia, but your talent is what's kept you here. I need to see if you're capable of continuing that without my guidance."

Ah, there it is—the dig.

It's true I got this job because of my uncle, but it's also true that I've worked my ass off to keep it. I'm a damn good social media manager. I work harder than anyone else in the department, come up with excellent content, and help keep a team of skilled members on task. Blake and I kick ass at co-managing, and I *love* this job. Being the social media manager for an NHL team is exactly what I want to do. Funny considering a few years ago, I couldn't even tell you anything about the game of hockey, but here I am loving every minute of it. I think I'm as in love with the game as I am with my job, and that's saying something.

Becoming the director of all media relations with an NHL team would be a dream come true. A dream I never knew I had, to be honest. Not until I got here.

Now, I want more. I'm ready for more.

I want that director position, and I want it *bad*.

"I am," I tell her. "I'm ready."

"It's going to mean longer hours, more time away from your family." Her eyes flick to Blake because we both know that's who she's talking to. Blake has a doting husband and a daughter.

Me? I don't have anyone, and everyone knows it. I'm alone, which is why I'm perfect for this job. I have plenty of time to devote to it.

"I understand," I tell her.

"Good," Tori says, sounding unconvinced. "As we start to prepare for another playoff run after Christmas, I'd like to do another player profile like we did last season." By *we*, she means the series Blake and I produced and she had zero involvement in. "The fans responded well to it, and I believe that's what drove our social media numbers up across the board in the last half of the season. I want to do that again. In fact, I want to *double* our numbers."

Double? Sure, we gained a lot of exposure last year with the profile we did on one of our most beloved players and his picture-perfect family, but to *double* that? We'd need a damn good piece...and possibly a miracle.

"I'd be happy to gather a list of potential subjects. I—"

"They want Smith," she states definitively.

It's three simple words, yet they are all it takes to make the hairs on the back of my neck stand straight up.

A chill runs down my spine, and I pray nobody notices my reaction.

I run my tongue along my rapidly drying lips. "Owen Smith?"

Her shrewd eyes narrow just a smidge, and I can tell the thin ice I've already been walking on has just gotten thinner. "Well, he is the only Smith on the team, so yes."

Of course she means him. I was just hoping that, by some miracle, another Smith was traded to the Comets and I missed it and she wasn't referring to one of the most underrated centermen in the league.

But nope, she means Smith.

My Smith.

I swallow thickly, and she doesn't miss it.

"Is that an issue?"

"Well, it's just that last year he refused."

She lifts a perfectly shaped brow. "Your point?"

"I just thought…" My words die when her brow rises even higher.

"Well, don't think. Just act. He's a mystery, and the fans want to know more about him. So, get him on board before the Christmas break."

My stomach drops. Not at her words—I am unfortunately used to those—but at her request.

I don't want to work with Smith more than I already have to, and working with him for the player profile series will require just that. Last year when we did it on a defenseman, I got close with not only the player but his wife too. We followed them the entire season.

Having to spend all my extra time with Smith...I'm not sure I can handle that.

"We will," Blake assures her, his knee knocking into mine again.

Kiss-ass.

But he's not. He's just telling Tori the truth that I can't handle. We *will* get Smith on board. We *have* to if we want this promotion.

And that sucks for so many reasons.

Tori focuses her attention on the pile of papers on her desk, and Blake and I are both aware that it means we're dismissed. We rise to our feet, our eyes connecting in a silent conversation of *What the fuck just happened?*

Tori doesn't speak until Blake's hand hits the door handle, and we both pause to look back at her.

"I trust you're both aware of what being a director means, yes?"

"Um...yes?"

She sighs, sitting back in her chair. "It means you're the media relations face of the team. It means *you're* the one who is setting the example. That sheet being passed around out there"—she nods toward the office—"means something different for you, something more. You'll do well to remember that if you want a thriving chance."

Blake and I exchange another glance, then nod frantically.

Tori looks away again, and we scurry from the office, both running scared.

"Are you insane?" Blake hisses the moment we're

down the hall and safe from Tori. "I can't believe you kept asking her to repeat herself!"

"I was shocked!" I argue back in a hushed tone. "I didn't think she'd ever quit. She gets off too much on being hateful to us all."

Blake cracks a smile. "That's fair. But that was the rumor I was going to tell you about." He shakes his head. "Good gravy, Em—I thought she was going to crawl over her desk and strangle you, and that would have sucked because I'm not sure I would have helped. I have a kid, and kids are expensive. I need this job."

"Gee, thanks," I mutter, pushing past him toward the state-of-the-art coffee machine we have. I press a button for a double espresso with steamed almond milk, then rest against the counter.

Blake settles in next to me. "Speaking of my job… you know I don't want that promotion, right?"

I nod because I kind of figured. It's demanding, and he already complains about missing time with his husband and their new baby. "I know."

"But I'll help you with the piece on Smith. Just when the time comes, the credit is all yours."

Smith.

The simple mention of his name has my body running hot.

"Hey, don't look so worried. It's going to be great. You're going to get the promotion. We'll make sure of it."

He doesn't understand. Not getting the promotion

isn't what I'm worried about. I'm an amazing manager. I deserve this promotion.

What I'm worried about is working with Smith. Because that new rule about not sleeping with the players?

I already broke it.

CHAPTER 2

EMILIA

Two & a half years ago

You know when you've had a long day at work and everything that could have gone wrong did, and all you want to do is go home, take off your pants, pour a glass of wine, and order a pizza?

That was all I wanted: pants off, wine poured, pizza delivered, in that order.

I definitely did not want to open my apartment door and find my boyfriend of three years plowing the single mom who lives next door.

And if that wasn't enough...the baby she's been taking care of by herself for the last year?

His.

That means practically from the moment we moved in together, he was sneaking around with her.

I'm a fool for not seeing it before now. All those times he went over there to help her fix something in her apartment? I thought he was simply being a good neighbor. I had no idea he was busy falling for her.

When he helped build the crib for her baby? I thought he felt bad that the dad wasn't around. I had no idea he was assembling furniture for his own child.

The worst part of it all? I *liked* her. I babysat for her! I helped buy diapers for her.

I am such an idiot.

The Dick Who Shall Not Be Named offered to let me have the apartment, but I couldn't stand the thought of living next door to them.

The whole thing felt like a sign, like it was finally time to move on from the small-town life and get out from under the boss I hated so much. So with the small savings I had in my bank account, I quit my job and moved to Bartlett. With a good word from my uncle, I was able to secure a social media manager position that gave me a very nice pay raise.

That's what I'm doing here tonight at some place called Slapshots—I'm celebrating.

By myself.

Because I left all my friends behind too, including my best friend, Hollis. So, that's why I'm currently sitting at the bar alone on a Friday night.

Whatever. At least I'm not sitting at home crying into my pint of Ben & Jerry's like I have for the last two weeks.

I take a sip of my whiskey sour and glance around. There are several smaller groups dispersed throughout the space as well as a large crowd around the other end of the bar. The music is loud, but not so loud you'd have to yell to talk to someone.

Not like I'm talking to anyone anyway.

I let out a long sigh. Maybe I should just head home. I'll lie and tell Hollis I stayed the whole time. She'll never know the difference.

My cell phone buzzes against the bar top.

Hollis: Don't you dare think about leaving.

I gasp, looking around, half expecting her to be in the bar somewhere.

Hollis: And before you freak out, no, I'm not hiding in the corner. I just know you, Em.

Me: I was totally thinking of bailing.

Hollis: I know you were.

· · ·

Hollis: Just stick it out. Even if you don't meet anyone, you can say you did it, and that will make next time easier.

Me: NEXT TIME?!

Hollis: Yes, next time. You're going to have to meet new people somehow.

Me: Can't I just wait until I start work next week?

Hollis: And do what in the meantime? Wallow in your new apartment? Not happening. If I were there (and I know, I know, I'M NOT), you know we'd be out on the town right now, prowling around the bars trying to get you laid.

Hollis: So that's what I want you to do. Prowl. Get laid. Forget about TDWSNBN (I motion to shorten that to just The Dick). Find someone who will rock your world for one night (maybe two if you're lucky) and be the badass bitch you are.

. . .

Hollis: Find a new dick to replace the old one.

I know she's right. I could easily spend another night buried in ice cream and watching movies that make me sob, but why waste the empty calories and energy on a man who didn't love me? I don't need to treat myself like crap just because he did.

The sooner I realize that, the sooner I can get back to being me.

Me: Motion approved.

Me: And you win. I'll stay.

Hollis: There's my girl!

Hollis: Now, push your shoulders back, lift that chin, and...wait, is there anyone sitting next to you?

Me: There's a girl on one side (gorgeous but I'm not into chicks) and the other seat is empty.

· · ·

Hollis: Good. You're going to flirt with the next guy who sits next to you.

Me: The very next one?

Hollis: Yep. No exceptions. If he's not your type, consider it practice.

Me: Okay. I can do that.

Hollis: YOU GOT THIS!

Hollis: And if you do go home with anyone...

Me: Turn on Find My Friends. I know, Mom.

Hollis: Love you.

Me: Love you more.

.   .   .

I set my phone back down on the bar.

That's when I notice someone's taken the seat next to mine.

He's not paying a lick of attention to me, his gaze wholly focused on the empty glass in his hand. He's older, a bit of gray peeking through the dark hair around his temples and in his beard. His skin is tanned, and there's a bump to his nose that makes it look like he's broken it a time or two. A scar cuts through his eyebrow, and I really want to reach out and run my finger across it.

Even with the imperfection in his brow and the frown pulling those thick lips down, he's still handsome.

You're going to flirt with the next guy who sits next to you. No exceptions. If he's not your type, consider it practice.

I take a steadying breath and decide to go for it.

"You know, my mama always told me if a man is frowning that deep, it means one of two things: he's had his heart broken, or his dick don't work."

"Excuse me?"

"I'm just repeating what she said is all."

I turn toward him and nearly gasp when I gaze into his amber eyes.

Oh…this man? He is *definitely* my type.

I don't even bother to try to hide my attraction to him, letting my tongue roll over my now drying lips.

"Though I'm going to guess it's not the latter."

He raises a dark brow. "That so?"

"Yep." I stick my hand out toward him, hoping it's

not clammy because *what the hell am I doing?* I push the insecurities away and say, "Emilia. And you are?"

He glances down at my outstretched hand like he's not sure if he should shake it or not. When he finally slides his palm against mine, I have to fight the shiver trying to work its way down my back.

"Smith."

CHAPTER 3

SMITH

"Dude, you look like you're trying to take a shit." A finger is pressed into my eyebrow, right into the scar I got when I was twenty-six. "Stop frowning. You're going to get more wrinkles, old man."

"Stop touching me, rookie." I smack his hand away and glare over at the obnoxious idiot sitting next to me.

His eyes narrow and he puffs his chest out indignantly. "I'm not a rookie anymore."

Fine, so Miller, a right-winger who has some of the slickest mitts in the league, has been with the Carolina Comets for a few years and is not technically a rookie, but he sure as shit still acts like one.

Can't say I blame him though. I did the same stupid stuff he's doing at his age. Going out partying, always a different woman on my arm—it's almost like a rite of passage in the NHL.

But I'm thirty-eight and too old for that crap.

"Compared to me, you just started skating yesterday."

He snorts. "I'm pretty sure compared to you, just about everyone in this league just started skating yesterday, Apple."

Apple. It's a nickname I both love and hate.

I love it because it represents my ability to set up my teammates on plays and earn a top spot in NHL history with the number of assists I've racked up over the years.

But I also hate it because it's a reminder of the years that are stacking up against me because it's not just Apple for assists. It's for *Granny Smith* Apple. They're calling me old, as if I don't fucking know it.

That sinking feeling of losing the game I love slips into my gut again. No matter how many times I try to shove it away, it slithers back in. The expiration of my contract with the Comets is creeping closer and closer. By the end of this season, I'll be an unrestricted free agent, and because of my age, it's a real possibility that the team won't sign me again.

I'd be lying if I said I wasn't scared that my time in the NHL is coming to an end, which means my chances of hoisting that Cup again are dwindling by the day. I don't know how to face either of those realities.

I'm lucky; I know that. Making it to the NHL *and* sticking around, especially as long as I have? It's a once-in-a-lifetime opportunity. Hoisting the Stanley Cup? Un-fucking-likely.

Having done it once, though, I want to do it again, and I want it *bad*.

This is exactly why I can't afford any distractions this

year. Hockey is my sole focus. It's the only thing that matters, the only thing that has *ever* mattered. And if I'm being completely honest, it's probably mattered a little too much sometimes. I've put all my time into the game. There's no way I'm going away without a fair fight.

"Seriously, man, what's with the shit look? You're supposed to be jazzed. We're playing hockey!"

Miller bumps his shoulder against mine, and I hate to admit it, but his smile is downright infectious.

We're on a five-game homestand, and so far, we've won every game. We have just two more to go before the short Christmas break, and then we're on a sprint for the playoffs. There is nothing like playing in front of a home crowd, especially when you're winning. The roar of your number one supporters cheering and clapping for you to win is incomparable. I much prefer it to being on the road for a multitude of reasons, but it all starts with the crowd.

"Just trying to stay focused," I tell him.

He nods. "I get it."

Except he doesn't. He's young. Barring any injury, he has many, *many* years ahead of him. Me? I know it's just a matter of time before I'm passed to another team for a yearlong contract...or not offered one at all.

I know some players are cool about it—anything to keep playing, right?—but I don't want that. I'd rather bow out with a team I love than play for one where my heart just isn't in it. I've watched too many good men fall to the wayside and have all their accomplishments turn to dust because they went out with a team where they weren't appreciated for the skilled player they were.

I refuse to let that happen to me. I don't want to be a forgotten great.

"Give the old man a rest, Miller," our goalie says. "*Wheel of Fortune* just ended. It's past his bedtime."

I glare at the smartass little shithead. He just started with the team at the end of last year, and frankly, he's a prick. Too fucking big for his pads, that's for damn sure.

But he's good. *Really* fucking good. Probably the best chance we have at winning the Cup this year. We didn't go down because of bad goaltending last year, that's for sure.

"I don't need you coming to my rescue, Greer."

He scoffs. "I think the words you're looking for are *Thank you.*"

I stare holes into his back as he shoves off of the bench, all his gear on and ready to go, then heads out to the hallway to join the other guys.

"Damn." Miller whistles lowly. "That guy is something."

I don't tell him he's also *something*, just a different kind.

Miller rises, then claps me on the shoulder. "See you out there."

I'm the last one out of the dressing room. Always am and always will be. It's my thing. Not a superstition, just a comforting sort of habit. I like to take a moment to clear my head with nobody around.

So that's what I do. I breathe in, then out. In and out. Rinse, repeat.

And I'm almost to that state of calm I like to enter just before a game when I hear a clicking sound, then a muttered, "Shit."

I whip my head up to find the one person I didn't want to see before the game, the one person I need to avoid if I'm going to have a distraction-free season.

"Sorry," she says quietly, that sweet voice of hers all too familiar to my ears. She wrings her hands in front of her, looking uncomfortable being alone with me. "I, uh, didn't mean to interrupt. I thought the room was empty." She lifts her phone. "Need to shoot some content."

"Your *uncle* send you back here?"

I don't know why there's venom lacing my words.

No...that's a lie. I know exactly why—she's the epitome of everything I want but can't have, and I fucking hate it.

The discomfort in her gaze is gone, and in its place is a glower that would make lesser men cower. "I don't need permission."

I try not to react to that because we both know she *loves* waiting for permission from me.

She steps farther into the room and begins snapping photos of some of the gear, ignoring me the entire time. I assume it's for some social media thing she has going on.

I know I shouldn't be sitting here staring at her, not when I have a game to go play and especially not when I can hear my teammates in the hallway going through

24

their pregame routines, getting ready to head down the tunnel.

But I do it anyway.

I trail my eyes from her long, toned legs over one of those hip-hugging skirts I swear are the only thing she owns, past her blouse that's unbuttoned just enough for me to see the swells of her breasts to the perfect pout of her full lips, which are currently trapped between her teeth as she concentrates on the task at hand.

She's gorgeous, and that's a problem.

It's a problem because I know what she feels like... what she tastes like.

Over two and a half years have passed since I've touched her, but somehow it feels like just yesterday, and my desire to do it again hasn't waned no matter how hard I've tried to stay away from her.

She inches closer to me. I'm not even sure she realizes she's doing it, but I sure as fuck do. The scent of fresh vanilla and lavender wafts toward me with every step she takes, and I'd be a damn liar if I said I didn't want to reach out and touch her.

But I can't.

I *really* fucking can't.

I shake my head and rise from the bench, needing to get out there for the game before I get my ass chewed or do something I know I'll regret.

The second I stand, she whirls around and realizes just how close she is. She takes a tentative step back, and

I don't blame her since I'm over six foot eight with my skates on. That doesn't mean I like it.

I match her step back with one of my own. She gulps, tipping her head back, all that gorgeous red hair of hers hanging down her back as she stares up at me with wide eyes.

That hair that looks good wrapped around my fist…

Those eyes that kill me…

I take another step toward her.

"S-Smith…"

But that's all she's able to say.

"Hey, there you are." Blake, one of the other social media managers, strolls into the room, not realizing what he just interrupted.

Really, I should thank him, because he just stopped me from doing something monumentally stupid that we agreed we'd never do again.

"Smith, you're just the man we're looking for. Did Emilia ask you about the player profile?"

I slide my eyes to Emilia, who looks like she wants to murder Blake right now. I kind of want to murder him too, but for different reasons.

I am *not* doing a player profile.

For one, I don't need people all up in my business. For two, I don't *want* to do it. I have more important shit to focus on than someone with a camera following me around trying to get a behind-the-scenes look into the life of a pro hockey player.

"Blake!" Emilia hisses, but he ignores her.

"Please tell me you're in," he says to me. "Because the fans voted, and they want you."

Last year they did a piece on one of our defensemen and his family. I know the fans ate it up, but I figured that was because you got to see it all—the wife, the kids…how he balances everything.

"They want me?"

He laughs, probably at how absolutely fucking shocked I am. "Yeah. Guess that whole quiet, brooding thing you have going on makes them curious."

Curious? I think he means nosy as fuck.

But I guess I get it to some extent, not being in the industry and being curious about how it all works. I'd probably be dying to know what it's like to play in the NHL too if I wasn't here.

But why *me*? Of all the players on our team, why pick me? I'm boring as shit. Old compared to the other guys. Single with no sordid past. I don't have a family, and my only friends are on the team.

So again…why me?

I look at Emilia, and to my surprise, she doesn't flinch under my heated stare.

Was this her doing? Because this definitely violates the whole *ignore one another and pretend it never happened* agreement we have.

As much as I'd like a repeat of our weekend together, it's not going to happen.

It *can't* happen.

She is off-limits for so many reasons, and that's

exactly why I'm going to stay away from whatever little project they want to try to rope me into.

"So, what do you say?" Blake asks, his blinding white smile pulling my attention from Emilia to him. "You game to let us follow you around for a bit, get some footage?"

"No."

His smile slips just a bit like he really thought he was going to get me to agree with just a grin. "Not even for the fans?"

"No. Now if you'll excuse me, I have a game to win."

Blake's jaw drops and he looks like he wants to say more, but I don't want to hear it.

I turn on my skates and head for the tunnel, but not before taking one last glance back at Emilia. She looks disappointed, but that's okay. I'm disappointed in myself too.

Because despite all the reasons I shouldn't, I still want her.

CHAPTER 4

Two & a half years ago

"You know, my mama always told me if a man is frowning that deep, it means one of two things: he's had his heart broken, or his dick don't work."

I glance over at the woman sitting next to me, two elbows laid on the bar top. She's stirring what looks to be a whiskey sour with one hand, and the other is fingering the small hoops lining her ear as if she didn't just accuse me of not having a working cock.

She's wearing an olive-green tank top and a pair of jeans that, if she were standing, I'm sure would be molded to her body. There's a mess of deep red hair pulled into a ponytail that hangs almost midway down her back. It's the kind of hair that would look damn good wrapped around my fist as I fed her my cock.

I give myself a shake.

I shouldn't be thinking those kinds of things about women I don't know.

"Excuse me?"

"I'm just repeating what she said is all." She lifts a pale, freckled shoulder, swiveling toward me on her stool, her bright green eyes startling me. Her gaze travels down my body, tongue poking out to roll across her bottom lip, liking what she sees. "Though I'm going to guess it's not the latter."

There's no hint of recognition on her face, but there is one thing that's abundantly clear—she's on the hunt.

And I just might be willing to get caught.

She's young, too damn young for me. I likely have at least ten years on her, and I don't have any business fooling around with someone like her.

But I can't seem to stop myself, especially not when she's looking at me like that.

"Smith," I say after she introduces herself, sliding my palm against hers, rubbing my thumb across the back of her hand. I lean into her, our hands still clasped. She doesn't back away. Instead, she scoots closer. "And I can assure you, *Emilia*, that my dick works just fine."

Her nostrils flare when I say her name. "Good to know."

"Is it?"

She nods, settling back on her stool. She lifts her drink to her mouth and runs her tongue around her straw, keeping her eyes on me the entire time.

Oh, I was right. She is on the hunt, and she's marked me as her prey.

That's fine. I'll play along.

"So, Emilia, do you come here often?"

"So cheesy." She shakes her head, finishing off her drink. "And no. This is my first time. I'm new in town—just moved here."

"You know, you probably shouldn't tell strangers you're new in town. If I were a lesser man, that would be an invitation."

"An invitation for what?"

"To do bad things to you."

She leans into me again. "What if I want you to do bad things to me?"

Now it's me whose nostrils are flaring, her words going straight to my—working just fine, thank you very much—dick.

"You're playing a dangerous game."

"Hmmm," she purrs, rolling her tongue over her lips again, knowing exactly what she's doing. "Is it dangerous if I want it?"

Rod chooses that exact moment to appear, dropping my Jim and Coke in front of me, breaking our spell.

He looks at Emilia, silently asking if she wants another drink.

"She'll take another," I answer for her.

Miller's beer is going to have to wait because there's no way I'm walking away from her right now.

A grin pulls at her plump lips, then she turns to Rod. "Whiskey sour, please."

He nods and turns to make her drink.

"So, new-to-town Emilia, what brings you all the way out here?"

There's a shift in her demeanor, her shoulders slumping just an inch or so, and the spark that was filling her vibrant green eyes has dulled.

Rod sets a new drink in front of her and disappears. Her fingers immediately find the straw, like she's searching for something to do with them.

"I...um...I needed a change of scenery."

"Ah. So you're just getting out of a bad relationship."

She laughs, then draws a long pull from her drink. "Is it that obvious?"

I shrug. "I'm just good at reading people."

It's a skill acquired from so much time on the ice— another reason the Cup loss sucks so bad. I should have read the other team better than I did, should have seen the play coming, but I didn't, and we lost because of it.

But I don't want to dwell on that now, not when I have such a beautiful woman sitting in front of me.

"What happened?" I ask.

She lets out a long, sad sigh. "The usual. Girl loves boy, boy says he loves girl, they move in together. You think things are fine, maybe even heading toward marriage. All the while he starts sleeping with the girl next door, fathers a child with her, and you don't find out until you find him plowing her on the coffee table." She snorts. "How they didn't break that thing is beyond me. That man's go-to move is the jackhammer—and he's not good at it."

"Wait—he had a baby with her?"

"Yep."

"And continued a relationship with you like it was nothing?"

"Yep. He said it was my fault because I was never home. Said if I had just tried harder in bed, he wouldn't have stepped out, and I should have been there for him more."

"And he's still breathing?"

"Unfortunately." She winces. "I shouldn't have said that. That was uncalled for."

The fact that she can find compassion for him after what he did…it does something funny to me that I can't quite explain. She's a good person. Better than me, that's for sure. I'd have beat his face to a bloody pulp and still not let up.

What kind of sad sack of shit does that? Who the fuck says those things to someone?

The smile that was lighting her face when she was flirting with me is gone, replaced by a frown that could rival mine. I want to see her smile again.

"Is that why you're here tonight? Trying to get over him?"

She nods, that hair of hers that I'm dying to unbind bouncing with the movement. "I promised my friend I wouldn't sit on the couch and wallow over The Dick anymore."

"The Dick?"

"That's what we're calling him. Hollis says he doesn't deserve to be named."

"Hm. I agree."

"What are you doing here? You were frowning an awful lot when you sat down."

"The same thing you are—trying to get over a heartbreak."

It's not entirely dishonest. I did get my heart broken. It wasn't a girl, but another kind of mistress—the game of hockey.

"Well, look at us." She stirs her drink again, her frown deepening. "Two peas, one pod and all that."

A silence falls over us, though it's not an awkward one. It's more of us both acknowledging what's happening here, the inevitable ending of tonight.

Right on cue, she turns to me, that grin back in place. "Want to get out of here, Smith?"

So, we do.

I usher her out of the bar, pulling out my phone to grab an Uber. The car arrives quickly, and we climb into the back. With one arm slung across the back seat of the SUV, I slip my phone into my pocket, watching as Emilia taps away at her own screen. Her hair is brushing against my arm, and I'm sure it makes me absolutely deranged to say the slight contact is making my dick throb.

It's been too long since I've taken a woman home, too

long since I've felt this sense of urgency, too fucking long since I've let myself go.

"I can feel you staring at me," she says quietly.

"Are you telling someone where we're going?"

"Yes."

"Good girl."

She swallows at my words, and I don't miss the way her thighs clench together.

"But I'm not worried." She slides her phone into the small crossbody purse she's carrying. "Not with you."

Unable to stop myself, I let my fingers tangle in her hair, grabbing a few strands. Her lips part when I give them a gentle tug. I wonder what she'd do if I wrapped them around my fist like I really want to. Would she moan? Would she beg me to stop? To pull harder?

"Why's that?" I ask.

"Because something tells me I don't need to worry with you."

I want to scold her for putting her trust in a stranger so blindly. I should tell the driver to turn around so I can take her back to the bar where she's safe. I should do a lot of things, but what I definitely shouldn't do is yank her close to me and cover her mouth with mine.

I do it anyway…and she lets me.

I have a feeling what we're about to do is going to ruin me.

CHAPTER 5

EMILIA

I knew getting Smith on board would be hard, but I didn't realize it would be *this* hard.

"Okay, is it just me, or is he grumpier than usual?" Blake shakes his head, staring after the player in question. "Sheesh. Guy needs to get laid or something."

"Blake!" I glance around the room, making sure nobody heard him. It's pointless. It's just the two of us in here, just like it was me and Smith alone in here.

It was dangerous being alone with him. I know that. The minute I saw him, I should have left.

But I didn't. I tempted fate, even though I know I shouldn't.

For starters, he's more than ten years older than me, and we are in two different places in our lives. I'm just getting settled in a career I plan to stay in for many years to come. His NHL career is likely coming to an end any time now.

Secondly, he's my uncle's player.

And finally, there's that pesky little rule about not

having relationships with the players. He's off-limits... even if I've already had him.

"What?" He shrugs. "It's true. He's always been a grump, but damn, that was probably the worst I've seen so far. That's saying something because we also work with Adrian Rhodes."

I can't help but laugh because he's right—Adrian "Beast" Rhodes is a notorious grump. He's even worse than Smith on a good day, but I can't exactly say I blame the guy. He has a long, nasty scar along his face from a hockey injury many moons ago, and it draws a lot of unwanted attention. Being a grump is his defense mechanism.

"You think maybe if *you* ask him nicely, he'll say yes?" Blake suggests as I continue snapping photos of the equipment. We're doing a before-and-after, behind-the-scenes look at the dressing room on our Instagram, and I wanted to get these taken quickly so I can get out there and watch the game.

"How would me asking him change anything?"

"I don't know. He seems to like you more than he likes me. He's always scowling at me."

"He's always scowling at *everyone*."

"Except you."

I pause at his words but quickly brush them away. He has no idea what he's talking about. Smith doesn't look at me any differently than anybody else.

I don't acknowledge Blake's accusation. Instead, I

snap one last photo, then turn his way. "I think we have everything we need for now. Let's go watch the game."

He narrows his eyes for only a moment, looking every bit like he wants to say something else but decides against it. That brilliant smile of his lights back up.

"You want me to go watch hot hockey players fly around the ice? Count me in."

The Comets are already five minutes into the second period when I am finally able to go downstairs. Usually, whenever I can catch games, I watch from the upper deck with the other staff members, but tonight Hollis is here with her younger sister, Harper, who just so happens to be married to Collin Wright, one of the defensemen.

"Oh, yay! You made it!" Hollis practically squeals as I plop down in the seat next to her. She wraps her arms around my neck and gives me a tight squeeze like she hasn't seen me in years even though I just saw her two days ago.

When I first moved out here from western North Carolina, I was sad. Not just because of my broken heart, but because I was leaving behind my best friend, especially since we'd been attached at the hip since first grade.

The last thing I expected was for her to follow me this way just two years later and end up pregnant by the team's captain.

"How's my baby girl doing?" I ask, placing a hand on her swollen belly.

She doesn't know what she's having yet, but I'm convinced it's a girl. Lowell knows, but he won't give any indication if I'm right or not.

She laughs. "Of course you'd ask about the baby first." She covers my hand with hers, gently giving it a squeeze. "We're good. Someone is just being a little sassy today."

"You or the baby?"

"Yes." She laughs again.

"I hope they got some good shots with Lowell and the bump."

"Always working." She taps her finger against the side of my head. "Shut it off. Enjoy the game."

"Yes, Mom." I roll my eyes. "Are you a hockey fan yet?"

She lifts her hand, shaking it back and forth. "Eh."

"She's here because she's horny and hoping to get laid. I know the look," Ryan, Rhodes' wife, says as she bounces her brows up and down. "Lowell is *so* getting lucky tonight."

"Stop it!" Hollis hisses, but she doesn't deny it.

"What? Hockey is *hot*! It gets everyone's panties wet."

The pink that fills Hollis' cheeks tells me Ryan is not far off the mark and that's exactly why she's here tonight. I really can't say I blame either one of them. There *is* something insanely attractive about the game. The

39

sounds, the way their bodies move, all the hot guys smashing against one another...yeah, I totally get it.

"You're terrible tonight," Harper tells her friend.

"Just tonight?" Ryan sticks her tongue out before turning back to the game.

I shake my head with a grin, shifting my attention to the ice just in time to see Smith jump over the boards and into the action. He slides into the other team's zone and effortlessly steals a puck, then whips it over to Rhodes, who tosses it to Wright. Then it's back to Rhodes and back to Smith again, and once more to Rhodes, who buries it on a one-timer.

The entire arena erupts in cheers, strangers high-fiving and hugging after the goal. The guys gather along the boards right in front of us, patting each other on the back and celebrating the first goal of the night.

Rhodes, knowing exactly where his girl is, looks over at Ryan and winks. It's cute because even though Rhodes is a huge, scarred, scary-looking guy—who is aptly named Beast—he's a softie for his wife.

Rhodes looking in our section pulls Smith's attention, and he glances our way too. His eyes collide with mine, and I suck in a sharp breath at the intense look he's shooting my way.

It's not anger. It's not elation. And it's not indifference. Whatever it is...I don't hate it.

But I'm not sure I like it either.

Our stare is broken when Wright bumps into him. Smith laughs at whatever he says, and they all skate away, ready to do it again. And they do, adding two more goals before the period ends, then another two in the third for good measure.

When there's under five minutes left in the game— which is my cue to get back to work so we can wrap up all our social media posts for the night and get home at a decent hour—I head back to the upper deck to find Blake.

He ends his conversation, and we head back to our offices just as someone scores to make the game six to two.

"Apple, Apple, Apple!" The slow, steady chant leaks out into the halls.

Blake chuckles. "You'd think with the way they're chanting his name, he'd agree to the video series. They obviously love him."

They really do, and he loves them too. This is why it sucks so bad to know the reason he's refusing the player profile is me.

I can't let that happen. There's no reason the fans should suffer because we can't be mature adults and move past...well, our past. I *have* to convince him, not just for my promotion, but for the fans. It's the right thing to do.

I only hope I can get him to see that too.

"Are you going out to Slapshots tonight?" Blake asks.

"I don't know..." I hedge.

I don't typically go out after games. I'd much rather head home, kick off my heels, and take a long hot shower because game days are long and tiring. If I do go out, I avoid Slapshots at all costs. There are too many hockey players and too many memories wrapped up in the place.

"You bailed last time, and the guys are on a hot streak tonight. Everyone's going to be there. Even me. Nate's insisting a let loose for a night."

I grimace because he's right. If I don't go tonight, my absence will likely be noticed, which probably isn't good if I'm trying to get a promotion.

"Come on," he pleads. "Say yes. Besides, I'm sure Smith will be there. Good opportunity to corner him for the piece."

Shit. He has me there. It would be a good chance for me to talk to him…especially since we'll be in the safety of the public eye. No room for us to not act like professionals.

"All right. Fine. Count me in."

After all, I have a player to bribe.

Luckily, by the time we get to Slapshots, the crowd is dwindling. I barely catch Hollis and Lowell as they're leaving—looking every bit as horny as Ryan said—and she promises to shoot me a text.

My first stop is the bar because I know I'm going to need a drink to be able to get through the rest of the night, especially if I'm going to have to spend any length of time in the presence of Smith and act like I haven't seen him naked.

I lift my hand toward Rod, the owner of Slapshots, who is always behind the bar on game nights. I think he loves the thrill of being able to serve the players himself. He nods, indicating he'll be over in a second, then heads to help another customer real quick.

I hop up on the stool, settling in because it might be a moment. This place, even though the crowd has definitely thinned, is still pretty busy. I glance around, spotting several players all over the bar, each of them broken off into their little groups, doing their own thing. The other patrons are so used to seeing them here that they don't even bat a lash or bother them. Either that or they're well aware that Rod isn't afraid to kick someone out for bugging them too much.

On my scan of the room, my gaze skates right over a pair of amber eyes I'm all too familiar with, then jumps right back.

Smith.

His gaze is locked on me, and I swear I can *feel* his stare raking over my body as if he were actually touching me. I wonder if he's thinking the same thing I am— about the last time we were in this bar together.

About the time we met.

About how I'd just moved to the city and went home with a stranger and spent two days having the most intense sex of my life only to find out he was a player for the team I'd just signed a contract with.

He has to be thinking about it too. There's no way he's not.

Not with the way he's looking at me.

I'm thankful I have my thick hair swept up in a bun because sweat breaks out across the back of my neck as he drags his eyes from my crossed legs, over my simple white blouse, to my face. His stare is so intense it feels like he's touching every inch of me, which is ridiculous since he's across the room.

He lifts his drink to his lips, drains the amber liquid, and then rises. Suddenly he's not safely across the room anymore—he's stalking across it…and heading for me.

I don't take my eyes from him as he practically glides through the crowd, his massive six-foot-six frame towering over everybody. His wide shoulders carve a path as he eats up the distance. He's changed into a pair of jeans that cling to his legs, showing off his strong thighs, and a simple dark blue Comets t-shirt with the number twenty-seven displayed on it. His dark hair is peppered with silver, his beard full but shaped cleanly, and it's so unfair because he's frustratingly handsome, the kind that *forces* you to notice him. It's intoxicating, and I'm buzzed just being in his presence.

He doesn't stop until he's sliding onto the stool next to me.

The moment he sits down, Rod appears. "Another Jim and Coke?" the owner asks.

Smith nods. "And a whiskey sour with a lime wedge instead of lemon."

He remembers.

Rod looks over at me and squints. I wonder if *he* remembers too. If he does, he doesn't comment, just says a quick "Coming right up" before he taps the bar twice and turns to make our drinks. He works fast and is sliding them across the bar top in under two minutes before hurrying off to help other waiting customers.

I sip eagerly at the sour mix, downing nearly half of it in one go before finally turning to Smith. I open my mouth to speak, but he beats me to the punch.

"What are you doing here?"

I snap my mouth shut. Is he serious?

My brows slam tightly together. "Last I checked, this is a free country. I'm allowed to be here just as much as you are."

He sighs. "Of course you're *allowed* to be here, but you're usually not. So, what are you doing here, *Emilia?*"

The way my name slides past his lips sends a shiver down my spine. I think since I've known him, he's only said it a few times, and never as intimately as he did just now.

When I don't immediately reply, he scoffs. "Let me guess—this is about the player profile thing?" He takes a sip of his drink, shaking his head. "You're wasting your time. It's not going to happen."

"And why not? The fans voted for you. They want that glimpse into your life. Are you really going to deny them when they give so much to you?"

"Are you guilt-tripping me?"

"Maybe."

Yeah, okay, so maybe I am laying it on thick right now, but I kind of need to. He *has* to agree to this because I want that promotion bad. If it means spending more time with Smith—which I really don't want to do —I'll do it.

I'm not going to let one weekend that happened over two years ago dictate the rest of my life. We need to move on from it.

"You know I'm right. You owe this to them."

He narrows his eyes at me. "Do I though? I put my body on the line every night for their entertainment. Am I really the one who owes them?"

"Yes, getting paid millions to play a game is such a hardship." I roll my eyes. "Look, can't you just agree? It won't take much time out of your schedule, and if it makes you feel more comfortable, I won't be the one following you around. I can have Blake cover it all. I don't think that'll go over well for the promotion, but we'll get it figured out in the end."

"Promotion?" His brows crush together, drawing my eyes to the scar that cuts through his right one. I never did get the chance to ask him how he got it, and I really want to know.

I nod. "Yeah. Tori's quitting."

"Oh, good. That lady scares the shit out of me even."

I laugh at that, considering how big and scary he is. But that just proves my point even more—Tori is terrifying, and she's not messing around when she says she wants Smith for this series. If I can't get him on board, I can kiss that promotion goodbye.

"So, this is why you want me so desperately? For a promotion?"

I choose to ignore his phrasing and the way it makes me feel. "Yes. It's my dream job."

"Funny, I seem to recall that you weren't even sure things were going to work out here for you."

I did tell him that back when we first met, and I meant it. I didn't know if uprooting my whole life was a good idea at the time, but I had to try it. There was no way I was going to be able to stay in that small town and face my ex and the woman he fathered a child with while we were together.

"A lot can change in two and a half years."

"Tell me about it," he mutters quietly.

We sip our drinks in silence for several minutes. Then several more minutes, and several more.

I have no idea how long we sit there, but the silence becomes unbearable, and I can't go another minute sitting in it.

"Are you really going to make me beg, Smith?"

His head whips my way, and I immediately regret my choice of words. We both know what happened the last time I begged him.

His eyes spark with a darkness I am all too familiar with, a darkness I yearn to awaken in him again, even though I have no business yearning for it at all.

I don't know how or when it happened, but we've

inched closer to one another...too close, dangerously so...yet neither of us makes a move to put space back between us even though we both know we should.

His eyes drop to my lips, then he slowly drags them back up, and the fire that's blazing in his gaze burns hotter.

"Smith..."

I don't know why I say his name. I'm not exactly sure what it is I even want.

Do I want him to kiss me?

Do I want to kiss him?

Yes.

The word whispers through my mind, even though it shouldn't, and I inch closer to him, even though I shouldn't.

"Can I get you another drink?" Rod asks.

We jump apart like we've been caught doing something we shouldn't, and quite frankly, we have. This bar is full of hockey players and other members of the staff—how could we be so careless?

Smith nods, and we don't speak until Rod slides fresh drinks in front of us.

The hockey player tosses his whiskey back, nearly finishing it in one gulp like he hasn't had a drink in days.

I don't touch mine. I'm not a big drinker, and I'm already feeling buzzed. I don't know if it's because of the alcohol or Smith. Either way, I should be careful so I can keep my wits about me.

"I'll do it."

His words are quiet, but they still cause me to jump, probably because his voice comes out all scratchy like he hasn't spoken in hours when it's only been minutes.

"Huh?"

"The player profile…I'll do it."

"You will?"

He nods. "But I have one condition."

Of course he does. "Name it."

"I want you."

My breath is stolen from my lungs with those three words, and my thighs clench together of their own accord. "E-Excuse me?"

"I want it to be you," he amends. "I don't want to have to answer questions, play silly games, and make ridiculous content and whatever else with some random person. I want it to be you."

"Smith…" I say quietly, and that's all I say because he knows what I mean.

It's a bad idea. Horrible, really. The worst damn idea he's ever had.

But he seems determined. I can see it in his soulful golden eyes.

"Okay," I relent. "Okay."

"Good." He nods. "Good." He clears his throat. "When do we start?"

I can't help but laugh at how pained the question comes out. "Well, we won't start filming anything yet, but I'd like to talk about what to expect with the series since it will last for the rest of the season. Perhaps we can meet after your morning skate tomorrow?"

He winces but nods again. "That's fine."

I know I'm asking a lot of him. Smith is a private guy.

"Thank you," I say softly. "It means a lot to me."

He glances down, and only then do I realize I've placed my hand on his arm. I yank it back quickly, like touching him is suddenly burning my skin.

Slowly, he drags his eyes back to mine. "For the fans."

I swallow. "For the fans."

Except it doesn't feel like it's for them at all.

This feels like it's for us...when we both know it can't be.

CHAPTER 6

Two & a half years ago

We ride the elevator up to his apartment in silence, much like most of our drive here was spent.

We don't need to talk. We both know what this is— one night together.

When we reach his floor, his hand falls to the small of my back as he steers us down the hallway. He doesn't stop touching me, not even when he slips his key into the door and pushes it open. When we cross the threshold, I take my first breath in what feels like hours.

I've never gone home with a strange man before. When I met The Dick, it was through a mutual friend, and we went on five dates before we went back to his place. Before him, I'd only dated two guys, and neither was serious.

This...this feels different than anything ever before.

"How old are you?" I blurt out.

"Thirty-six."

Holy…

"How old are you?"

I wring my hands. "Twenty-six."

"Christ," he mutters, and I'm sure he's thinking the same things I am.

He's ten years my senior.

He's too old for me, much more experienced.

And yet, I don't care.

I step toward him, reaching out and fitting my hands around his massive biceps. "I want this."

He screws his eyes shut tight like he's warring with himself over this new revelation.

Just when I think he's about to shove me away and call me a ride, his hands find my hips, and I hear him mutter, "Screw it."

Then his mouth is on mine.

The kiss is searing, and I swear I feel it down to my toes. His mouth ravages me, taking control and kissing me hard. Our tongues tangle together, and it's wet and hot and everything I could have hoped for.

Before I know it, my back is pressed against a wall, and Smith is right there, shoving a knee between my legs. One hand cradles my head, the other digging into my waist, fingers beginning to dip into the waistband of my jeans.

He trails his lips down my chin, over my neck, nibbling and sucking at me until he reaches the swell of my breasts. When he realizes my shirt is in the way, he wastes no time peeling it off before placing me right back where I was. He buries his face in my chest, kissing at all the exposed skin before pulling a cup of my bra down.

He doesn't ask. Doesn't hesitate. Just covers my nipple with his mouth and sucks hard.

He uses his teeth and his tongue to tease until I'm pulling at his hair, needing him to move or do something else because I need something else. He catches my drift… and moves directly to my other nipple. He teases me just the same, pulling me to the edge of frustration before finally popping free.

With one hand, his eyes on mine, he undoes the button of my jeans, then slowly peels the zipper down. Just like before, he's touching me without any preamble.

His hand slides into my jeans and inside my panties. He grazes over my clit, causing me to moan in pleasure, but he doesn't stop. No—of course he doesn't. He doesn't quit until he has one finger pumping in and out of my drenched pussy.

He's not inside me long before he pulls his finger free.

"Oh god," I cry out. I can't tell if it's from pleasure or the pain of being so close to the edge and getting backed away yet again.

Then he's pulling my jeans down my legs, only stopping to slide my shoes from my feet.

I'm standing before him in nothing but my underwear. My tits, swollen and wet, are hanging out of my bra, and there's an obvious wet spot on my panties.

"Almost there," he mutters, stepping into me.

He reaches up and pulls the ponytail holder from my hair, letting my long, red waves cascade around me. He steps back to admire his work, palming his hardened length through his jeans.

"Fucking perfect."

His eyes slowly rake over me, taking in every single inch until I'm squirming beneath his heated gaze. There's a fire in his eyes burning so hot I'm certain I'm going down in flames as I stand here.

"Do you like sucking cock, Emilia?" he asks quietly.

I swear my mouth waters at just the thought of it.

I nod, licking my lips.

"On your knees, then."

I don't argue. I drop to my knees, already knowing I'm going to love the sting I'll feel on them tomorrow, and watch as he strips his shirt over his head, then undoes the button on his pants. He drags the zipper down, frees his cock, and waits.

When I reach forward for him, he shakes his head.

"Put them behind your back."

I do.

"Good. Now come here."

I scoot closer, the roughness of the tile edges digging into my skin.

"Open up, Emilia."

I drop my jaw.

"Good girl."

He guides his long, thick cock to my mouth, running the head of it back and forth along my tongue. I can already taste the saltiness of his pre-cum—and I already want more.

He gathers my hair up with one hand, pulling it tight and tipping my head back.

"I'm going to fuck your mouth. If at any point you want to stop, just grab my leg. Understand?"

I nod.

"Use your words, Emilia. I need confirmation."

"I understand."

"Good girl," he says again, and I love the words just as much as before.

He makes good on his promise. He pumps his cock in and out of my mouth, slowly at first. Then, his movements get bolder...deeper. So deep he prompts my gag reflex a few times. When I react, he backs off, waiting for me to tap out.

I never do.

He pushes to the back of my throat over and over again, sometimes holding himself there, seeing how much I can take. I have no idea how long we do this for, how long he fucks my mouth, but I love every single second of it. I just wish I could touch myself; I'm aching so badly, need the release more than I've ever needed one in my entire life.

Like he can sense it, he pulls off, and we're both gasping for air.

"Need to fuck you," he says, pulling at my hair, tugging me off the floor.

He presses me face-first against the wall, pushing my

hands flat and pulling my ass out.

"Don't move."

I wouldn't dare.

I listen as he rustles around in his jeans, then wait as he rips open the condom. He grunts as he slides it down his length. I can't see him, but I hear him move his hand over his cock a few times before I feel the blunt tip against my entrance.

He leans over me, his lips at my ear. "By the time I'm done with you, you're going to forget all about him."

I'm almost embarrassed by the whimper that leaves my lips as he presses into me slowly.

"Oh shit. You're so fucking perfect," he whispers, sliding into me inch by sweet inch.

When he's to the hilt, he pauses, letting me adjust to his size, then he gently begins rocking into me.

So...damn...slowly.

He pulls out until just the tip of him is inside me, and then he slams back in. I gasp at the pain that's quickly overtaken by pleasure burning through my veins.

Smith chuckles, then does it again. And again. He wraps one hand around my hair, tugging at me until my head falls back and his lips are on my ear.

"I'm really going to fuck you now, Emilia. Are you ready?"

I nod because it's all I can manage.

He pounds into me again and again and again, so hard and so fast I'm up on my tiptoes, clawing at the wall, needing a reprieve. I'm torn between wanting to run away from him and wanting to push back and meet his thrusts. Something tells me all I need to do is stand right here, letting him use me.

And fuck, does it feel good to be used like this.

Out of nowhere, my orgasm hits me. It's so hard and intense as stars explode behind my eyes, and I think I might even stop breathing for a moment.

Suddenly I'm being spun around, my legs wrapping around his waist, and I'm thankful for it because I'm not sure I'd be able to stand much longer. Smith carries me down a dark hall into what I assume is his bedroom. He drops me onto the bed, then crawls between my legs, wraps one around his waist, and slides home again.

"Oh!" I cry out when he hits that spot that drives me wild.

He slams into me again, and another whimper leaves me. His thumb finds my clit and he rubs at it in short, rough circles.

"I can't," I tell him.

There's no way he's going to make me come again. I have literally never orgasmed twice during sex.

"You will," he instructs, leaning down to take my mouth with his.

He slows his pace, kissing me softly and sweetly, a vast contrast to how he was just fucking me. It doesn't take long until I'm approaching the edge of that cliff again.

He smiles against me when my hips begin to move on their own, thrusting up to meet him. "I told you so."

He pushes back to his knees and looks down at me

with a hunger I've never seen from someone else before. He's looking at me like he can't get enough, like he'll never get enough.

And I'm not sure I ever will either.

I didn't get a good look at him before, but god, he's perfect. The moonlight from his open windows casts beautiful shadows across him. His muscles are tight and defined, his chest full of hair I bet would feel good beneath my cheek.

His hips snap into mine as he pounds into me. The moment his thumb finds my clit again, I'm seeing stars for the second time tonight. He laughs darkly, but it's short-lived as his own orgasm races through him. He stills above me, looking like absolute perfection with his head thrown back mid-climax.

When he finally comes back to earth, he grins down at me and collapses into a heap beside me. Our breaths are coming in harsh. I have never had someone fuck me so thoroughly before, never had someone know exactly what I needed without having to tell them.

I've never wanted to do it again so damn badly.

I hear Smith pull off the condom and toss it into what sounds like an empty trash can, then he falls back beside me. After several minutes—during which I'm certain he falls asleep—the panic begins to set in.

I've never done this before. I've never had to deal with the aftermath of a one-night stand. Do we cuddle? Am I supposed to grab my clothes and leave? Do I leave my number? I have no idea.

I go to push off the bed, and a giant hand lands on my stomach, halting my movements.

"I...I should go," I say quietly.

"Why?"

"Because isn't this just a one-night thing?"

"Yes."

"Then I should leave."

He tugs at me, pulling me back to him, and I let him. He rolls until he's on top of me, staring down at me with those golden-brown eyes as he stretches my arms above my head, locking his fingers with mine. "Do you want to leave?"

I tuck my bottom lip between my teeth, contemplating that.

Do I *want* to leave? No.

Should I leave? Yes.

"You're a lot older than me," I say.

"I know."

"And I don't know you."

"You don't." He presses a kiss to my nose. "That's all stuff we can figure out later. We're not discussing it right now. Right now, I'm asking you...do you want to leave?"

"No."

"Then stay. We can figure the rest out."

I chew on my lip again. He leans down, sucking my lip into his mouth, soothing away the ache I've caused. When he pulls back, he's looking at me with that same heat I saw earlier.

That same heat I feel pooling in my lower belly once more.

That same heat I'm certain is going to leave burns.

"Stay," he says again.

And for some crazy reason...I do.

CHAPTER 7

SMITH

I have a few tendencies toward select kinks, but I've never considered myself a masochist until yesterday. Why the fuck else would I agree to a player profile *and* ask that Emilia be the one to do it?

I'm an idiot. There's no arguing that. I just agreed to spend my free time with the one person I shouldn't be spending *any* time with. But the way her bright green eyes lit up when she was talking about the promotion…I couldn't tell her no. The word was right there on the tip of my tongue, but instead, it came out *I'll do it.*

I'm playing with fire; I know that. I just can't seem to stop.

"I heard you got roped into doing the player profile this year." Rhodes laughs, shaking his head. "What a fool."

"Dude, no shit?" Collin says, eyes wide with surprise. "I can't believe they got you of all people to agree. You're just as private if not worse than Lowell and Beast over here." He motions toward Rhodes, who smacks his glove away.

"Don't say that like it's a bad thing. Not all of us enjoy getting arrested and having our faces splashed across the media."

"I didn't enjoy getting arrested." Collin pauses. "Well, okay, I might have enjoyed the handcuffs a little, but that's all. Besides, you're one to talk about drawing media attention, Mr. Get Drunk-Married in Vegas."

Rhodes scowls at his friend as he skates away to practice his shots, and I laugh because he's not wrong.

While we normally do tend to keep a lower profile than some of the teams out there—they have guys with some very public and nasty relationships—something has definitely been up with the Comets the last few years between Collin's arrest, Rhodes' very public marriage, and Lowell getting his one-night stand pregnant.

Collin turns to me. "But seriously, man, how did they convince you to say yes? I saw all the silly shit they had Woody doing last season. I can't believe you'd agree to that."

I try not to groan because I am not looking forward to some of the stuff they did. Most of it's harmless, like FAQs and fill-in-the-blank type of shit. What I'm not looking forward to is sitting down and spilling my guts to a camera for hours, mostly because I'm not sure I'm ready to face the reality that I have nothing outside of hockey.

"It was voted on by the fans," I say in way of explanation.

"Shit."

Shit is right. For the most part, the guys on the team are good about doing any sort of public event and interacting with the fans, even those of us who are known for being hard-asses on the ice. We know we owe it to them, so we suck it up. But to willingly put oneself front and center like this? It's a fool's gamble.

"How'd they even get your name in the nomination pool?"

It's the same question I've been asking myself, because I sure as hell didn't sign up for anything.

"Well, about that..." Miller says, coming to a stop behind me.

I glower at him. "Please tell me you're kidding and this wasn't your doing."

"I'm kidding?" I take a step toward him, and he holds his hands up. "Hey, in my defense, I didn't think anybody would actually vote for you." He winces. "Okay, fine, so not a lot of people actually voted for you."

"I don't know if I should be offended by that or not."

"Definitely offended," Miller clarifies. "I just figured, you know, you're old and single and have like zero friends. You need to get out there, live a little. Maybe one of our single lady fans will hear about your sad excuse for a love life and take pity and finally get you laid. So I made a bunch of fake accounts—which is like super easy to do when you have money and can pay someone to do it for you—and had 'them' vote for you."

My glare intensifies, but he doesn't care.

"You can't be mad at me," he continues. "I saw you and Emilia at Slapshots last night. It didn't look like you were trying too hard to say no to her."

I'm genuinely shocked I didn't see him, because when Miller is somewhere, you typically know he's there. "You were there?"

He shrugs. "Yeah, I was playing pool in the corner with Greer." He dips his head toward the man in the net who blocks the shot from Rhodes effortlessly, which is damn impressive because Rhodes has a wicked wrist shot.

"If you wanted to score with the ladies, why didn't you sign yourself up?" Collin asks Miller.

"I can't be the main event all the time." Miller grins, but it's not the same confident expression he usually wears. It's almost like something is hiding behind it.

Hmm…

"If I knew that hot redhead from the social media department was spearheading the whole thing, I definitely would have because"—he lets out a low whistle —"*damn.*"

My blood simmers hearing him talk about Emilia in any capacity, but it really starts to boil over when I see how serious he is. I might have no business fucking around with her, but I don't want Miller going anywhere near Emilia either.

"Dude, shut the fuck up." Collin shoves him. "You know that's Coach Martin's niece, right?"

It's the reminder I need but don't want. Knowing Emilia is our assistant coach's niece has been the only thing keeping me away. It's wrong on too many levels, and it's a line I wouldn't be able to uncross.

Collin shoots his eyes across the ice to make sure nobody heard, but we're in the clear.

"Really? But she's so hot, and he's so...not."

"Shut up, Miller." Collin rolls his eyes. "And maybe don't be saying that shit out loud. There's a strict *Don't fuck the staff* rule."

"There is?"

Collin rears his head back, surprised by my question. Hell, *I'm* surprised by my question. I shouldn't care because nothing is going to happen between us.

"Yeah..." He says it slowly, studying me too closely for my liking. "Did you not read the memo they sent out yesterday?"

"Huh," I say, turning my attention back to practice. "Must have missed it since it doesn't apply to me."

"Right," he mutters, but he doesn't sound all that convinced.

The truth is, I'm not convinced either.

"Smith!"

My head snaps up upon hearing my name, especially since it's Coach Martin calling for me. That same feeling of unease that always passes through me when I have to talk to him hits again. It's been that way for two and a half years now, and I wonder if I'll ever get used to it.

I skate over to him. "What's up, Coach?"

His gaze is focused on the net where Greer is still working to block shots. "How's he doing?"

"He's good. Solid. Rebounds could use some cleanup, but good."

Coach crosses his arms over his chest, eyes still on the ice, watching people fly around. "And how do you think the team is playing in front of him? Confident? Stilted? We don't need another Daskin debacle."

I know he's asking me because I've been with the team the longest and played in front of the most goalies out of anyone here.

Right now, he's referring to our goalie from about eight years ago, who was great. We went far because of him. But…the team was also *too* reliant on his skills. It might be a goalie's job to stop pucks from going into the net, but if your team isn't defending its zone, it's not going to matter how damn good your goalie is.

That year with Daskin…it took us entirely too long to figure that out, and we bombed the next season after making it all the way to the Cup final the previous year. It was like we all just lost our ability to gel together.

"I think we could be a little faster on our skates, block a few more shots," I tell him honestly. "But mostly solid. As long as we don't get complacent, I think we'll be good."

Coach nods. "I think so too." He taps his elbow

against mine. "Heard you're working with my niece for that big interview thing they do."

My mouth goes dry at the mention of Emilia, and before I even try, I know I'm not going to be able to form any coherent words, so I nod.

"She's a good kid. I never had any of my own, but she's always felt like mine, you know?"

I don't know, but I don't tell him that.

"Proud of her. She's accomplished a lot since she's been here."

His lips are pulled into a wide smile, his eyes taking on a shine, and I want to punch myself in the face because I'm standing here listening to him praise his niece and pretending I don't know what she looks like with my hands in her hair and my cock down her throat.

I swallow back the unease trying to climb its way up my esophagus. "She seems...lovely."

Lovely? Fucking hell, Owen.

His smile widens. "She is." He gives his head a shake. "Anyway, I'll let you get back to practice. Just wanted to get your opinion. You're our most veteran guy, and we trust your gut instinct. We know you'll never do us wrong, Smith."

I give him a tightlipped smile before skating away, feeling like a complete and total dirtbag and once again asking myself, *What the hell did I get myself into?*

I pull open the door to Cup of Joe's and immediately spot Emilia at the back of the small coffee shop that's a favorite local hangout spot. She must be listening for the chime of the door because she whips her head up at the sound and a bright smile curves her lips.

I'm taken aback by it. She's never once looked at me like she is now.

She must be thinking the same thing because it quickly transforms into a frown. And then it goes somewhere in between the two as she lifts her hand in a tiny wave.

It's cute. *She's* cute.

I point toward the coffee bar in a silent question, and she nods. I step up to the counter and place my order for a small black coffee for myself and another medium coffee with cream and three sugars, just how she likes.

"Sure thing," the barista says, running her tongue over her lips, eyes raking over me. "Anything else I can get you?"

"A muffin and a slice of banana bread too."

"Sure." She bites her lip. "*Anything* else?"

"Nope. Not a thing."

Her shoulders deflate at the brushoff, and I can't help but laugh. Puck bunnies, man.

When my order is up, I balance the drinks and plate together and make my way over to the small table Emilia's secured.

"Thanks," she mutters as I sit down.

"No problem." I point to the plate. "Feel free to eat

whichever. I like both."

"Me too."

"Split them?" I suggest, and she nods.

I rip each one in half, then slide her coffee her way and watch as she takes a tentative drink. Her eyes widen when she realizes it's right, and she gives me that same impressed look I got last night when I remembered she likes her whiskey sour with a lime wedge instead of lemon.

"This is perfect. Thank you."

"You already said that," I say.

Her cheeks turn pink. "Well, apparently I meant it, then." She flicks her eyes over to the coffee bar. "Make friends over there?"

I tip my head, studying her. "Jealous?"

She narrows her eyes, and I grin.

We sip our coffees and pick at our pastries in silence. That seems to happen with us a lot—silence. I'm not sure if it's because we don't have anything to say or if we have too much of it.

Her fingers go to the gold hoop dangling from her ear, and she tugs on it, looking anywhere but at me. It's the same set of earrings she was wearing the night we first met.

"Did you wear those on purpose?"

My words catch her off guard, and her eyes flash to mine with confusion. I nod toward where her fingers still play with the jewelry.

"O-Oh," she murmurs, dropping her hand into her

lap. "I… No." But she doesn't sound sure about that at all.

She reaches into her bag where it sits next to her and pulls out a tablet. She clicks around a few times before leveling me with an annoyed stare. "Let's start by going over some questions you don't want to answer."

"I don't want to answer any of them."

She ignores me. "Well, you don't have a wife or children, so we can skip those." She reads over her list. "We can skip that too…and that…and—"

"What's the point of this player profile again?"

"It's for the fans to get to know you and the game better."

"Right, but it's obvious we can't even use half the questions, so what's the point? Why me?"

"I don't know. Maybe because they admire you? You're a veteran player and—"

I snort. "*Veteran player.* That's the polite way to say I'm old as shit."

She quirks a brow. "You might be old*er* than other players, but it doesn't make you any less than them."

I gnash my teeth in an attempt to push away the argument that's clawing its way up my throat. I *am* less than them, and that's the problem. It's what my agent called to talk about on the ride over here, putting me in a damn sour mood.

"You're getting up there, Smith. I know you're focused on making the playoffs right now, but you need to face the real possibility of not playing for the Comets next year."

70

Like I don't fucking know all of that already.

But he's right about one thing—I *am* currently focused on making a run for the playoffs. I don't care about my contract expiring. I can't, not right now.

"You have an incredible stats sheet," she continues. "Not to mention you've been with the Comets all your career, which is something most players never experience. I think it intrigues people. They want to know what keeps you here."

Fear of change. Fear of screwing up my routine. Fear of being a failure somewhere else.

But I don't say any of that.

Instead, I tell her, "I like it."

Her green eyes bore into me like she's trying to reach inside my mind and pull out all of my truths. But if she can see through my bullshit, she doesn't call me on it.

"Right." She clears her throat. "Are you comfortable talking about your childhood? Our audience tends to like to know how far back your interest in hockey goes, but if it's an uncomfortable subject for you, we can skip that."

"I'm fine to talk about my childhood, but it might be boring. There's not much to tell."

Her brows crinkle together. "Why do you say that?"

"Because it's true." I shrug. "I grew up pretty privileged with a nanny, Bessie. She was the one who took me to and from the rink every day and made sure I got to practice and games on time. She's the reason I got into hockey like I did in the first place. Her brothers played and it was a game she loved, and she passed that on to me since I spent so much time with her. My parents would have preferred I go into a sport that's 'much more civilized,' as they put it."

A soft smile plays on Emilia's lips. "Is Bessie somebody we can interview for the profile?"

"She passed away about five years ago."

Her smile fades, and I hate the pity that replaces it. "I'm sorry."

I shrug again. "It's life."

"Actually, that—" She cuts herself off with a shake of her head. "Never mind. Not appropriate."

"No." I sit forward. "What were you going to say?"

She sighs. "I was going to say it kind of explains a lot about you."

I tip my head. "How so?"

"Well…" She lifts her shoulders, then gestures toward me. "The whole loner thing you have going on."

I force myself not to grin. "My loner thing?"

"Yeah. It's not exactly a secret that you're a perpetual bachelor. If your parents weren't around to show you real love and take care of you, it makes sense that you are not…romantically inclined."

"Thanks for the psychology lesson, Professor Anderson," I mutter.

I've already sat down and analyzed my childhood. My parents might not have been around often, but big whoop. It's not like I went without love. I had Bessie. I had hockey. Both loved me, and I was good.

I *am* good.

"I found my great love, and I don't need another. Hockey is it for me."

She pouts. "That's kind of…sad."

"Sad?" I wave my hand around. "I get to play the greatest game on earth, and I get paid to do it. Do I look sad?"

"Yes."

Her immediate answer makes me pause because it seems so genuine…and probably because she's not entirely wrong.

She leans forward. "Aren't you lonely, Smith? In the last few years alone, several of your teammates have met the love of their life and gotten married. Don't you want that for yourself? Someone to spend your time with when you're not on the ice? Someone to go home to after away games?"

Yes.

I do want that. I don't know when it snuck up on me that I do. Maybe it was seeing Collin and Rhodes find love, and hell, now Lowell too. Maybe it's just me getting older and wiser. I don't fucking know.

I just know that yeah, I am lonely.

But I'm not going to admit that to her.

"Aren't *you* lonely?" I toss back.

"Of course I'm lonely. But I…" She runs her tongue across her lips, her gaze landing just over my shoulder, lost in a trance…or a memory. Her gaze snaps back to mine, then she shakes her head. "But I can't have the things I want, so I accept that."

"Why are you letting yourself be lonely?"

"Why are you?" she throws right back at me.

I smirk. "I asked you first."

She sighs, crossing her arms over her chest and sinking lower into her seat. "You know why," she whispers.

"Do I?"

She glares at me. "Seriously, Smith?"

"Yeah, seriously." I match her heated stare with one of my own.

"Are we ever going to talk about what happened between us, or are we just going to let it be this huge elephant in the room? Because I'm honestly not sure I can work like this all season long."

"What's there to talk about? It was just sex. You were on the rebound, and I was sad about a Cup loss. That's all it was—sex."

The moment the words leave my lips, I regret them.

It wasn't just sex. I know that, and based on the sharp breath she takes in, she knows that too.

But maybe if I pretend it was, she will too, and we can get through this whole thing unscathed. At the end of the day, there's nothing either of us can do about it, and the sooner we accept that, the better.

"Fine." She shoves her tablet into her bag, then rises. "I'll be in touch about when we can meet next. Thanks for the coffee."

She turns on her heel, then walks away from me.

And I let her leave all over again.

CHAPTER 8

Two & a half years ago

I'm usually not one for sleepovers.

Sex is just sex. I get off and I move on. There are no attachments to it. There are no feelings. It's just an act, a release. Every person I'm with knows the score.

But last night when Emilia was about to sneak away, I had this sudden urge to keep her here.

It was alarming at first because it's a sensation I've never experienced before. I tried to ignore it, but as she slipped to the edge of the bed to leave, it grew, and I realized it was because something about her leaving just didn't feel right.

So, I asked her to stay, and she did.

Waking up next to her this morning, I know I made the right call. She's still fast asleep with her head on my chest, and part of me wants to wake her up so I can devour her all over again, slower this time, but I'm also enjoying watching her sleep way too much.

God, I can't believe I brought somebody home from Slapshots. It's like my number one hookup rule—no Slapshots. It's a hockey bar, and a well-known one at that, which means the people in there know hockey and who the players are, which means the women are there on the prowl. As a good rule of thumb, I avoid puck bunnies at all costs. Nothing good comes from a puck bunny.

But there was no hint of recognition on Emilia's face last night. She didn't look at me any differently than if I were just some random guy. I knew she had no clue who I am, and as shitty as it sounds, I kind of want to keep it that way for as long as possible.

We didn't exchange any info last night aside from our names, though technically I wasn't even truthful about that since I gave her my last name. But it was a test, and she passed.

I like that she passed.

I peer down at her as she sleeps soundly against me. Her lips are slightly parted as she breathes a steady rhythm. Her red hair is a mess and all over the bed. She has one hand clutched to my chest like she's holding on to me.

I don't know anything about this girl other than that she's ten years younger than me, but there's something about her that makes me want to know everything she has to tell me.

I don't get that feeling very often. Hell, I'm not sure I've *ever* gotten that feeling before, and that's exactly why I asked her to stay.

She wiggles against me, and I can tell she's stirring awake. Her legs stretch out and she does this cute little fluttering kick, and I know the exact moment she realizes she's not alone and is attached to a stranger.

I watch as her eyes open and she takes in her surroundings. She seems uncertain at first, but then last night hits her, and she seems calmer.

It takes another few moments for her to actually look at me. When she does, there's a small, tentative smile on her lips. I kind of love that she's nervous about this because deep, deep down, I'm nervous about this too.

"Hi," she whispers.

"Hi," I repeat back.

The softest giggle leaves her lips, and I'd do anything to hear that sound again.

"Last night was…nice."

I lift a brow. "Nice?"

Another giggle. "Okay, maybe a little *more* than nice."

"Maybe a little more…" I shake my head, then grab her by the waist and pull her until she's lying on top of me.

She gasps, laughing. "Smith! What are you—"

I tug her down, pressing my mouth to hers, not giving a shit about morning breath as I kiss her hard. Her laughter turns to moans and soon she's writhing against me, the evidence of what my kiss is doing to her obvious as her wet pussy slides against my stomach. She moves her hips, seeking the friction I'm offering.

I wrap one hand in her hair and the other gently around her throat, applying just enough pressure to both spots. I pull her back, watching as she rubs her pussy against me.

"Is this *a little more than nice*, Emilia?"

She nods, her teeth sinking into her lower lip.

"God, you're fucking beautiful," I mutter, dragging her to me for another hard kiss.

She doesn't slow her movements, using me to get herself off.

I love it, but I want more.

"Do you want to come, Emilia?" I ask against her lips.

She moans at my words. "Please, please, please."

Laughing at her begging, I drop my hands from her throat and her hair, and she slows her ministrations, her eyes flickering open at the loss of my touch.

"Up," I instruct.

"Up?"

I nod. "Stand up."

She does, and I scoot until my back is resting against the headboard and her cunt is right there, ready for me.

"*Fuck*," I curse when I see how wet she really is. Her pussy is glistening, and I know she was close just from rubbing herself against me. I *need* to taste her. I didn't get to last night, and something tells me she's going to be sweet.

"Use my tongue."

"W-What?" she sputters.

I don't answer her. I just simply open my mouth and flatten my tongue. Her eyes spark with understanding, and slowly, she bends her knees, pressing her cunt against it. She sighs the moment we collide, and I was fucking right. She's sweet, perfect.

And mine.

She fucks herself against my tongue, one hand on the wall, the other on my head, holding me to her as if I could possibly want to be anywhere else.

I don't. I could stay here forever and never get tired of the way she tastes.

She's close, but I can tell she's holding herself back. I want to make her come so I can bury myself inside of her and then do it again. I slide my hands up her legs, using one to steady her and the other to slip two fingers inside of her without warning. She cries out, her knees nearly buckling when I hook them, rubbing that spot I know she loves.

"Oh shit," she screams.

Then she's falling over the edge, her pussy clenching around my fingers, drawing them deeper as she works her clit against me still. I watch her fall apart, her head thrown back, and it's beautiful.

She's beautiful.

I don't even give her a chance to let the quakes subside before I'm tossing her onto the bed, pulling a condom from the nightstand, and covering myself. I don't give her any warning before I sink inside of her.

"Holy shit," I murmur, dropping my forehead to hers. "You're so fucking tight, Emilia. I fit inside you perfectly."

She hums a pleasured noise as I pump into her. "So perfect."

I try—like really fucking try—to take it slow, but I can't. She feels too fucking good. I fit my hand around her throat, loving the whimper that escapes her as she wears my hand like a necklace, and I break.

I pump into her hard and fast. There's no real rhythm, no finesse. It's pure, raw fucking.

And it is so damn good.

"Touch yourself," I command.

Her eyes find mine as she slides her hand between us and starts rubbing slow circles on her clit.

"God, you're perfect. You're doing so good," I say, and her eyes spark at my praise, spurring her to rub faster.

Her pants grow louder, her breaths coming sharper and sharper, and I know she's close. I tighten my hold on her throat and she falls apart, her tight cunt squeezing my release out of me as I fill the condom, pretending it's her.

I drop to my elbows, cradling her head and kissing her slowly and softly, a stark contrast to how I just used her. When I finally pull away, she's grinning up at me, looking spent and satisfied.

"So, uh, what's for breakfast?"

Laughing, I slide off her and drop the condom in the trash can by my bed, then turn back around. "Do you want to order in?"

She nods, and we spend the rest of the day in bed.

It's late Sunday night, nearly midnight, and though I've asked Emilia several times if I can drive her home, she refuses. Which is why I'm standing outside my apartment building on the sidewalk, waiting for an Uber to show up and take her home. I clutch her closer to me, keeping my arms locked around her, and she squeezes me back just as fiercely.

I feel so stupid for wanting her to stay.

All we've done over the last two days is stay hidden inside my apartment. We've ordered in for every meal, watched my favorite movie, *Point Break*, and hers, *The Princess Bride*, and have fucked on just about every square inch of every surface in this apartment.

More than that, we talked. A lot.

We talked about her douchebag ex and everything that happened with them, and it took every ounce of willpower I had not to hop in my car and drive across the state and beat his skull in for hurting her.

I told her about my secret love of puzzles and showed her my collection. After laughing at me and calling me an old man for it, she forced me to start one with her. We didn't get far before our clothes wound up on the floor again.

She told me about how she wants to vacation in Europe for two weeks and gave me a very detailed plan of everything she'd go see and do and how this new job of hers came with a big pay raise, so she might actually be able to afford it soon. I had to fight the urge to get on my phone and book her dream vacation right then and there because that trip is nothing but a drop in the bucket for me.

We talked about so much but still left out so many simple details. It's the lightest I've felt in years, and not just because of the sex.

The sad part is, we both know when she leaves, whatever magical bubble we've been living inside for the past two days will burst.

I can ask her to stay. I can ask to see her again. I know that.

I also know if she wanted to stay, she would. She's been using this weekend to escape reality just as much as I have, but tomorrow's Monday, and we have to go back to that reality at some point.

My heart climbs into my throat as the Uber pulls up to the curb.

This is it.

And for some reason, I don't *want* this to be it.

I think if we were in different places in our lives, if she hadn't just gotten out of a bad relationship and if I didn't have hockey front and center in my life, we could make something work.

But we do have those things, so this is it for us.

"Thank you for this, Smith," she says quietly.

Owen. My name is Owen.

I want to scream it at her.

But I don't.

"Thank you, Emilia."

She swallows thickly, then pushes to her toes, and our mouths collide for the last time.

It's not a rushed kiss. It's sweet and slow, and I take my time remembering every single moment of it.

"Uh, not to like interrupt or anything, but I'm here for Emilia?" the Uber driver says, *definitely* interrupting.

Emilia laughs against me, and the moment is broken. I place one last soft kiss against her lips before taking a step away from her, tucking my hands into my pockets so I don't reach out for her and steal her away back upstairs to our little haven.

A smile pulls at her lips, and she tips her head, studying me. She opens her mouth to say something but thinks better of it.

I pull open the car door for her, and I'm hit with panic.

"Wait! Your number. Give me your number."

Her face falls. "Smith, I—"

"I want to make sure you get home okay, and I'm not taking no for an answer."

She contemplates it and I know she wants to say no, but I'm praying she doesn't.

"Okay," she agrees quietly.

She picks her phone up and taps open the keypad so I can punch my number in. When I hand the device back over to her, I don't let her take it immediately.

Instead, I tug her back in.

"Smith…" She breathes out against me. "I have to go."

"I know." I nod, swallowing down my pleas for her to stay. "I know."

With one final kiss, I let her walk away.

The Uber pulls onto the street, and I have no idea how long I stand there watching. It's long enough that the taillights have been gone for what feels like hours before I finally force myself back into my building. I don't even bother with the elevator. I take the stairs, deserving the punishment for letting her go like a fool.

As I reach the final step, my phone buzzes in my pocket, and I scramble to check it.

Unknown: Safe at home.

Unknown: Thank you again for this weekend. Thank you for giving me a safe place to hide. You'll never know how much it meant to me.

· · ·

Unknown: Good night, Smith.

Her last two words are final, and I can read between the lines enough to know that our bubble? It burst.

And because I know I shouldn't, I don't text her back.

CHAPTER 9

EMILIA

It would be an absolute lie if I said I didn't come into work yesterday morning with every intention of telling Tori there was no way I would be able to do the piece on Smith.

But I knew if I did, I would have to explain to her why I couldn't do the piece...and that's not a conversation I'm ready to have.

Besides, letting him win and get the better of me? Well, that's just not the type of person I am.

Just sex? Just sex my ass.

He knows as well as I do that those two nights we spent together meant a whole lot more. If they didn't, we wouldn't have spent the last two-plus years doing everything in our power to avoid one another.

Maybe it's all in my head though. Maybe it was *just sex*. Perhaps my fascination with him is because he's off-limits. Maybe *I'm* the one who needs to move on.

I need to forget about what happened, forget about

SIN BIN

him in any capacity other than hockey. I have a job to do, and that's what I need to be focusing on.

"Hey, how's everything going with Smith?"

I sigh as Blake rests his ass on my desk, the same spot he always sits in.

"Uh-oh. That bad?"

"Let's just say it was a grumpy day for him."

"Isn't it always a grumpy day for him?"

"True, but when we met for coffee, he was *extra* grumpy."

Blake obviously doesn't know the details of my past with Smith. *Nobody* knows them, not even Hollis. She knows I met someone when I first moved here, but that's it. She doesn't know who it was because I didn't even know who he was then.

When we discovered he played for the Comets and I'd just accepted a job with them, we cut off all contact and have existed in this weird plane of avoiding one another ever since. Now though, we can't, and I'm beginning to realize it's going to be a lot harder to collaborate with him than I anticipated.

Blake frowns. "Well, at least he said yes. I mean, that's the first big hurdle, you know? And if he gets too out of line, you can just tell your uncle and he can whip him into shape."

I laugh. "Right. Tori already hates me for nepotism. The last thing I need to do is sic my uncle on an unruly player. I can take care of it. I'm not scared of Smith."

Though this would probably be a lot easier if I were...

"If you need help, just let me know. I've been working on my dad voice, but Nate says I could use more practice on it, so if I need to bust it out on some hockey players, I'll do it."

I laugh again. "I'll keep that in mind."

"Good, good. But also, while I'm here..."

I groan because nothing good *ever* comes after he says that. "Oh god."

"It's nothing awful. We're just down a photographer since it's so close to the holiday..." He pauses when I glare at him because I know where this is going. "Everyone else is wrapped up in their own projects, so we don't have anyone to photograph the arrivals. I'd do it, but Tori has me working on something else and she's already mad at me for dipping out early yesterday, so..."

He grins broadly, and I want so badly to say no, but I know I can't.

I sigh. "Fine, I'll do it—but I'm not going to be happy about it."

"I really didn't think you would be, but it's been noted." He pretends to scribble a note onto his hand, then hops off my desk. "I'm off to get these graphics made before puck drop."

"She has you on graphic duty? But that's..."

"Totally not my job? I know, but I think she knows I hate it, so here I am." He rolls his eyes. "Thanks for helping out. I'll let Dom know you're on your way down."

I hit save on the project I've been working on, then rise from my desk and head for the equipment room. I grab a camera and make my way down to the garage.

It's still sunny out, so I decide to take some pics of the guys coming in from the lot.

The minute I step outside, I regret it. It's windy as hell, and it sends a shiver through me. I should have known better. December around here can be unpredictable, freezing cold one day, warm and sunny the next. It's definitely sunny, but that wind chill is killer.

Nevertheless, I have a job to do, and the team is starting to arrive. I lift the camera just in time to see Miller and Rhodes making their way into the building.

Miller blows the camera a kiss.

Rhodes—who is scowling per usual—smacks him in the back of the head.

I laugh as I take the shot because the moment is just too good to pass up.

A few more guys arrive, including the goalie, Greer, who has been making a splash on our social media lately. Everyone in the comments has been going nuts over him and his skills. I'm eager to see how well he does in this last stretch of the season.

I lift the camera to my eye to adjust a few things, then spot Smith pulling in at the other end of the lot. He backs into a spot, then shuts off his shiny black truck and hops out with a coffee cup in hand. I don't know if that's a requirement before the game, but it seems like it since all the guys carry one in.

His dark hair is pushed back off his head in a haphazard way, and his face is covered with at least two days' worth of stubble. He's wearing a navy suit with a simple white dress shirt underneath. His tie is dark red, and even though it's not the most noteworthy ensemble, he sure wears it like it is. The outfit looks every bit like it was tailored to fit him, and I don't mind it at all.

He looks good. *Too* good.

Like a-tightness-pulling-low-in-my-belly kind of good.

Someone clearing their throat draws my attention, and I nearly jump when I see Lowell through the lens, standing just a few feet away. He looks behind him at Smith—who is making his way through the lot—then back at me, and his lips pull up into a knowing smirk.

I hate it and want to hide.

My cheeks warm ten degrees. "Evening, Lowell."

"Emilia. Lovely view out tonight, yeah?"

I let out a low squeak at being caught and called out, and Lowell laughs, shaking his head.

"Don't worry…your secret is safe with me."

"What secret?"

He just shakes his head again, smirk still in place as he disappears into the building. Panic sets in the moment he's out of sight.

Did Smith tell him what happened between us? Did Lowell guess himself? If so, does it mean it's obvious to everyone else? Does Tori know? Is this some kind of test?

No. There's no way. Smith and I have barely been in the same room since I started with the team. It's just not possible for her to know anything.

I shake the worry off and turn my attention back to my job. Wright jogs over toward Smith, and the two bump fists as they head for the building together. I can't make out what they're saying, but whatever Wright says has Smith's lips tipping up into a smile. He doesn't do it often enough, and it's a shame because he's even more handsome when it happens.

The wind whips up again, and I shiver from the onslaught.

"Here you go, Miss Anderson," says Dom, one of our security guards, as he slips his jacket over my shoulders. I relish the warmth, tugging the material around me together.

I shoot him a wink. "You're my hero, Dom."

His cheeks pinken and he returns to his post.

I lift my camera and grab a few shots of Wright and Smith walking in but stop short when I realize Smith's eyes have shot my way. His brows are drawn tightly together as he glowers at me with a hateful stare. He's looking at the jacket draped over my shoulders like it's the most offensive thing he's ever seen.

His eyes flick to Dom, then back to the jacket, then to me.

It's almost like...

Holy shit. He's jealous.

A warm tingle hits my lower belly when I meet his tawny eyes, which are dark and stormy. I want to walk over and smooth the crease between his brows...but I also want to make it deepen.

How messed up does it make me that I like seeing him jealous?

Beside him, Wright is carrying on a full-blown one-sided conversation, missing the whole thing completely.

I don't. I press the button and capture the shot as he stares at me, the intensity never waning.

When I drop the camera, Smith's attention is back on Wright, and it's like it never even happened. It's such a sudden change that even *I* question if it was real.

But then Wright notices me and grins, Smith scowls his way too, and I know it was real.

"Hey, Emilia. You're still coming for Christmas dinner, right? Harper's been freaking out about the menu and worrying if she bought enough food."

"I'll be there after I stop by my uncle's," I promise.

Since moving out here, I've taken to having Christmas brunch with my uncle. He's all alone since my aunt died six years ago, so I like to spend the holidays with him.

"Christmas dinner?" Smith asks the defenseman.

"Yeah. Do you want in? The more the merrier. Just figured your grumpy ass wouldn't want to hang out with us."

"I'm in," Smith answers quickly.

Wright's brows shoot up along with mine.

He's going to be there? How is it I've avoided him so much for the last couple of years and now suddenly I have to spend all my free time with him? And why don't I hate the idea of it?

"You are?" Wright asks him with a grin.

Smith lifts his shoulders. "Sure. Why not? Not like I have anything else to do."

"All right. I'll tell Harper. Bring booze."

Smith grunts out a reply, and I snap another picture as they pass, not missing Smith's eyes sliding my way as he disappears into the building.

I stand outside for another half hour as the rest of the team filters in, then I head upstairs to get the photos loaded into the shared folder so the graphics gurus—tonight that's Blake—can get them edited and ready for posting before puck drop.

I click through the images, checking to make sure everything came out okay, and I pause when I get to the ones of Smith.

God, the look he's giving the camera...I should be embarrassed that it has my thighs clenching together, but I'm just not.

Even though I shouldn't, I love seeing him so riled up over me. It reminds me of the nights we spent together, the intensity, the possessiveness. I've never felt so important to someone before, and though it was short-lived, I want to feel that again.

I click away before I get caught daydreaming, then

save the photos to the folder and get started on wrapping up everything else I need to do before the game. When I'm satisfied that it's all complete, I head down the hall and pop my head into Blake's office.

"Hey, I'm going down to the game," I say. "You coming?"

He's fully engrossed in whatever is on his phone, but after a few seconds, he pops his head up, eyes wide. It's alarming.

"Everything okay?" I ask hesitantly, hoping it's not a fire I need to put out. All I want is to go watch the game and relax tonight.

"Have you seen the comments on these?"

"On what?"

"The arrival photos. Look."

I slink into his office and stand behind his desk as he pulls up the team's Instagram on his computer. He expands the comments, and my mouth slackens at what I see on the screen. There are hundreds of them, way more than we typically get, and they all say a variation of the same thing.

HoneyBree19: Granny Smith Apple? More like DADDY Smith Apple.

Bardown1991: THAT LOOK! *fans self*

. . .

HckyisLife: Dude, Smith looks READY to go!

KeepingUpWithKeeley: I don't even watch hockey and here I am in the comments.

AmberWavesofFAME: I wish my husband looked at me the way he is looking at whoever is behind that camera. He's giving MAJOR BDE. *eggplant emoji*

CldBURStckHndlr: WOW. I'm pretty sure if he looked at me like that, there's no way I'd be wearing panties for long.

"They all need a large glass of water because they are *thirsty*. I mean, not that I blame them, because that photo is *wow*."

"What picture did you post?" My heart is pounding so hard I pray he can't hear it or the waver of my voice.

He clicks through the carousel of photos, but he doesn't have to tell me which one it is. I already know.

It's the same photo I was clenching my thighs to just a little bit ago.

The fans aren't wrong—the look he's giving the camera is panty-melting. Thank gosh none of them know it was me behind the lens.

"What did you do to him? Did you say something?

Because he's looking at you like he wants to rip your clothes off."

Probably because he does want to rip my clothes off, Dom's jacket in particular.

But I don't tell Blake any of that.

Instead, I shrug. "I don't know. He was just grumpy. You know how Smith is."

Blake's brows rise. "Honey, that look he's giving you…that isn't just him being grumpy. There is some *serious* sexual tension hiding underneath it."

His words spark a panic in me, and I look around the office to make sure nobody was walking by when he said that. The last thing I need is a bunch of rumors being spread.

"Shh!"

"What? I'm teasing! Unless…"

My blood is pumping so hard I can hardly hear the lie tumbling from my lips. "Don't be ridiculous. He has no interest in me. He was just annoyed with something Wright was talking his ear off about."

It's easily the biggest lie I've ever told Blake, and I immediately feel bad about it. But right now, this lie is what's saving my career. I just hope Tori doesn't see these photos, scrutinize them too closely, and start putting two and two together.

Blake's eyes narrow, and for a moment, I'm terrified he's going to press me and all the sordid details are going to come tumbling out because I am *dying* to tell someone.

By some miracle, he lets me off the hook. "All right.

But I'm just saying…Stick Handler here is right. If Nate looked at me like that, I would not be wearing pants for long."

He laughs, and I force myself to do the same.

"Okay, come on," he says, clicking out of the account, then rising from his chair. "Let's go watch the game and hope the boys win, because I do not feel like staying up all night and monitoring our social media for the crazies."

I breathe a sigh of relief as I follow him out. At least for now, my secret is still safe.

CHAPTER 10

"Last home game tonight, boys! Let's fucking win this!" Miller slams his shoulder into mine, jostling me on the bench, then darts away before I can retaliate.

It's funny how we all have different ways to prep for games. Mine is to be alone with my thoughts. I like the solitude of it all.

Miller, on the other hand, is that guy who needs loud music blaring and even louder conversations. He's the one running around the dressing room, bouncing on his heels with excitement.

Most days I can tolerate it, but tonight? Tonight, I want to rip his stupid phone from the charging dock and toss it across the room so the incessant Christmas music he insists on playing stops. I want to tell him to shut up, and I really fucking want to get back out on the ice already and land some hits.

It's all because I'm pissed.

I'm pissed because I let myself get upset about Emilia wearing somebody else's jacket.

I'm not stupid. I'm sure she's been with other people since we were together. There's no reason for her not to. She's gorgeous, and how anyone can resist her is beyond me. I've accepted that.

But seeing it? Man, it blows.

Of course the moment I walked through the door and realized it was likely Dom just being a gentleman, I felt like a fucking fool for having any sort of reaction to it at all. I'm almost forty years old for shit's sake. I shouldn't be getting *jealous*, especially not over someone who isn't mine.

That happens with Emilia a lot though. I do things I shouldn't be doing.

I wish I could get her out of my head. I wish I could forget anything happened between us.

But I can't, and that's the problem.

"You good?" Lowell asks from beside me.

I peek over at him and nod. "Yeah, I'm good."

His dark brows shoot up. "You sure about that? You don't seem good."

"I said I'm fine."

"No, you said you're *good*. There's a difference between *fine* and *good*. If you had ever been in a serious relationship, you'd know that."

I don't point out that up until he got Hollis pregnant, he had only been in one "serious" relationship himself. Now he's talking to me like he's some fucking expert. Funny for a guy still denying he's even in a relationship.

"Shut up," I mutter.

He laughs, then looks around to make sure nobody is paying us any attention and leans in. "This have anything to do with the woman behind the camera today?"

I don't even bother acting surprised by his words.

Lowell isn't stupid. I'm sure he's picked up over the years that something is off with Emilia and me, especially over the summer at Harper and Collin's wedding when I was having a weak moment and spent far too much of the night staring in her direction.

Yes, it has everything to do with her, I want to scream. *She's suddenly everywhere, and it's driving me insane.*

"It's nothing," I tell him instead.

"You can talk to me, you know. I'll totally braid your hair while we swap secrets."

He grins at me, and I shake my head, laughing.

It might sound like he's joking, but I know he's being serious. While I trust every member of this team, if I were going to spill my guts to anyone, it would be Lowell.

"Meant to tell you…I texted Harper before the game and told her you're in for Christmas. She's excited you're finally joining us," Collin says, dropping down beside Lowell, adjusting his elbow pads while we wait for the second period to start.

I try not to groan at the mention of the Christmas dinner I agreed to. I have no idea why I even said yes.

Okay, that's a lie. I know exactly why I did.

Emilia.

I have no business going, but I want to because now that I've spent time with her, I want to do it again.

Maybe my masochistic streak runs deeper than I realize.

"You're coming to Christmas?" Lowell asks me, a stupid fucking smirk ghosting across his lips.

I glower at him in response.

His smirk turns into a full-blown grin, and I already know I'm going to regret going to this damn meal because I just know he's going to be giving me that same ridiculous smile the entire time.

"I can't wait," he says, his eyes sparkling with mischief.

Yeah, me either.

It's a good feeling to win a game no matter what, but to win our entire homestand? Fucking amazing.

Sure, we still have the second half of the season, but getting these points early lets us breathe just a little easier. We've been playing hard, and tonight we played even harder. Our defense was top-notch, and our goal-scoring was even better. We walked out with a five-to-nothing win.

We're officially on Christmas break, and despite how I felt before hitting the ice, I feel like I'm flying right now. On a total high from a good game, I take my time standing under the hot water to help work out the soreness I'm definitely feeling from a hard checking game against Chicago.

Much like I enjoy being the last in the room before a game, I like being the last to leave after, so by the time I turn the water off, it's just me and two other guys left. One wraps up his post-game routine and gives me a wave before heading home to his wife and three kids, and the other is Greer, who looks like he's about to take off too.

"Nobody to run home to, old man?"

I glare at him because he knows nobody is waiting at home for me.

Miller invited me out to Slapshots tonight, and for a moment I consider taking him up on it just to show this little prick that I do have plans. Then I think better of it. I'd rather just go home and get a good night's rest. We're leaving right after Christmas for a six-game road trip, and if I'm not sleeping in my bed for that long, I'm getting as much time in it now as I possibly can.

And I don't give a shit how old that makes me sound.

He laughs, then stuffs the last of his things in his cubby. "See you after the break, Apple."

It's very bah humbug of me, but I flip him off behind his back. Feeling satisfied, I finish getting dressed, then make sure I have everything before finally heading for the parking lot. I round the corner to leave—and run smack into someone coming the opposite way.

I reach out to steady them, and only then do I realize it's the last person I'm expecting to see tonight. I drop my hands and she takes a step away from me, and I fucking hate that she does it.

"Smith," she says, sounding like she's out of breath. "What are you still doing here?"

"I'm always the last to leave," I explain.

She nods, glancing left and right, likely checking to make sure nobody is sulking around. "I'll make a note of that for the player profile," she teases. She clears her throat. "Good game tonight, by the way. Not far into the season and you're already racking up those assists, Apple."

I don't hate the nickname as much coming from her, and that's because she genuinely means it. She's not poking fun at my age or anything else; she's actually excited about my accomplishments.

"Thanks," I murmur.

Then, we stand there awkwardly. Neither of us makes a move to say anything, but we're also not running to get away. We're just standing here. I stare down at her, and she meets my stare with a steady one of her own.

And then all at once, we both start talking.

"So I—"

"Listen, I—"

We laugh, and I motion for her to go first.

She looks unsure as she brushes her long red locks from her face and rolls her tongue along her lips, taking a deep breath as she shoves her shoulders back.

"I want to apologize for what happened at the coffee shop yesterday, for bringing up our...*history*. It was unprofessional, and I shouldn't have done it. We've been doing a good job of pretending it never happened, so there was no reason we couldn't have kept doing that, no reason for us to keep dragging it up. You were right—it was just sex."

Her eyes flick away at her last words, and she folds her arms around her stomach, almost like she's protecting herself. I don't like it. I don't like her walking around thinking that weekend meant nothing to me. It did—a lot more than it probably should have.

Before I even realize what I'm doing, I haul her farther down the hallway until I'm certain we're alone. Then, because I can't fucking help myself, I box her in with my arms. She peers up at me with wide eyes, her gaze growing dark and her breaths coming in short spurts like her lungs are hungry for air.

"W-What are you…"

"I lied."

"W-What?"

"I lied. What I said yesterday…I lied." I lean into her. "It wasn't just sex, Emilia."

"But you said—"

"I know what I said, and I fucking lied." She gulps at the harshness of my words. "Do you really think I could just forget our weekend together? Do you really think there is any possible way I can look back on that and think it was *just sex*? After knowing what you feel like…" She sucks in a sharp breath. "Taste like…it's impossible."

She's panting now, her eyes full of confusion and lust and so many other emotions that I'm sure match what's in my own gaze.

"It was never *just sex*. It'll never be *just sex*. I wish it could be. I really do." I drop my forehead to hers. "Because I can't forget you, Emilia. No matter how hard I try…I can't."

Her breaths come in sharp, and I can feel them ghosting along my lips.

Half an inch…that's how close I am to tasting her again, and I want to taste her again so damn badly.

Her breasts brush against my chest with each heavy inhale she takes, and I have to try hard to convince myself to not press my body against hers. If I do, I'm a goner.

"Owen…"

My head snaps up.

She said my name.

It sounds stupid, absolutely ridiculous, but I've always been Smith, never Owen.

It's just four letters, but they roll off her tongue like a poem, and it's the best one I've ever heard.

I like it. Entirely too much.

I lean into her, and that familiar scent of lavender and vanilla fills all my senses, making my mind spin with the memories of before. Of her naked. Of her on her knees. Of her spread across my bed as I devoured her.

I want it all again.

There's a distant *thud*, and we're so lost in our own little world that it sounds a million times closer than it likely is. Whatever it is, it's enough to break whatever is happening between us.

Her tongue slides across her lips again and she looks up at me, so much regret in her eyes for the words she hasn't even said yet but that I know are coming.

"We can't."

Two quiet words that sound like an anvil dropping.

I could kiss her. I could kiss her, and I *know* she'd kiss me back because she wants this too.

But...she's right. We can't do this.

Because if we do this, I won't be able to stop. Not when I know how good we can be together.

So, I don't.

Instead, I push off the wall, creating space between us that I wish didn't have to be there. She stays with her back pressed against the wall, her chest heaving up and down like she's breathing for the first time in hours.

"I..."

I shake my head, cutting off whatever it is she's about to say.

She nods, rolling her tongue across her lips again and pushing off the wall. She runs her hand through her hair, straightens her blouse, and then slips past me.

I don't move.

I don't even watch her leave. The click of her heels against the floor is the only indication I have that she's stopped.

Quietly, she says, "Good night...Smith."

I hate that I'm no longer Owen.

CHAPTER 11

EMILIA

I almost kissed Smith.

It's been two days and I can't forget about it. I should have seen that coming though. It's been two years since I slept with him, and I can't forget that either.

My focus was shit as I tried to wrap everything up before the short Christmas break, and it sucked when Tori had to pull me out of my daydreaming more than once. I couldn't help it though. All I could think about was how close I was to throwing away everything I'd been working so hard for.

He consumed me. That scent that's all of him invaded every inch of me, and I didn't even want to take my clothes off when I got home, afraid it had seeped into them and I was going to lose it somehow. I should have known better because even now, I swear I can still smell him.

Just like I can still clearly see the swirls of yellows and browns in his eyes as he peered down at me. He was giving me the same look he did two years ago when I was on my knees for him, a look I wouldn't mind seeing again.

"Doing all right, Em?" Uncle Jared asks, brows drawn tightly together as he stares at me, face full of concern.

"Huh?" I shake my head, tossing away the thoughts I shouldn't be having, *especially* not when I'm in my uncle's home. I hope he doesn't notice the red in my cheeks. "Sorry, yeah. I'm good. Just tired."

"Tori working you hard, eh?" He laughs, rinsing off a dirty plate. "That woman is…intense."

"Don't I know it."

He doesn't even know half of it. I'm thankful for this short Christmas break not just because I get a break from Smith, but because I get a break from Tori and her watchful eyes.

"I heard she's thinking of having you take over as director…" He peeks up at me, and I can clearly see the pride in his eyes. "That true?"

"It's true. Well, me or Blake. Though Blake isn't really interested."

He nods. "Because of Nate and that adorable new baby of theirs. I understand that. The NHL is demanding, and it's different when you have kiddos involved. Speaking of…"

He laughs when I groan.

"Come on, kid. You can't hide behind your job forever. You have to get back out there sometime."

My uncle thinks I'm still hung up on my ex. And I

guess in a way, I am a little bit. I'm a lot more guarded and a lot less likely to give my trust away so easily, but that's not the reason I'm single.

"I'm focusing on my career right now," I tell him.

Which is the absolute honest truth. When I first got here, I was overwhelmed by everything that went into the social media aspect of an NHL team. It's not an easy job by any means, and I knew I needed to prove I didn't just get the job because of my uncle. I busted my ass, and I continue to bust my ass because I love doing this, being part of something bigger.

Am I lonely? Sure. Would it be nice to have someone to come home to at night? Of course, but I'm just not in a place for anything serious. I have too much on the line to let myself get distracted by dating.

My phone buzzes against the counter, and I reach for it, looking for any chance to get out of this conversation.

Harper: Don't forget a small gift for the exchange, and please remember to bring your choice of booze!

Lowell: Please bring booze because I'm going to need it. I'm meeting Hollis' mom tonight.

Harper: Oh, hush. She's not that bad.

· · ·

Miller: Wait…

Miller: We have to bring our OWN booze? But Wright makes more than all of us! Make him buy.

Rhodes: Nah. Lowell's got him beat by half a mil.

Lowell: Damn right I do. Makin' them big bucks, baby.

Miller: Going to need them for that kid you have on the way too.

Wright: Can we NOT talk about our AAV?? It's Christmas and I don't want to embarrass the rookie.

Miller: I AM NOT A ROOKIE!

Wright: Then stop acting like one, dipshit.

Harper: Stop the name-calling. It's mean.

· · ·

Wright: Yes, ma'am.

Miller: Getting kinky, huh?

Rhodes: It's not mean if it's true. The kid is a dipshit.

Ryan: Be nice, Adrian.

Miller: Oooooh, she first-named you. You hate your first name.

Ryan: He doesn't ALWAYS hate his first name. *evil emoji*

Miller: He loves it during sex, doesn't he??

Wright: Shut up, Miller.

Lowell: Shut up, Miller.

. . .

Rhodes: Shut the fuck up, Miller.

I laugh as the last three messages all roll in at the same time. Miller is a well-known shit disturber among the entire staff, so none of this surprises me at all.

"That your friends?" my uncle asks as he finishes loading the dishwasher.

"Yes. They're mostly just yelling at Miller."

"That kid." He shakes his head. "He's something else."

"That's one way to put it."

"But an incredible player." My uncle looks at me. "Don't tell him I said that though. It'll go straight to his head. We're trying to keep him knocked down a peg or two."

"My lips are sealed."

"Good." He winks. "Are you heading over to Wright's house for dinner?"

I nod. "Yes. Ms. Kelly will be there. She's meeting Lowell for the first time."

"Still can't believe that whole ordeal," my uncle mumbles. Then he tips his head toward the door, grabbing a dishtowel and drying his hands. "Go have fun with them. No sense in you hanging around here with me all day. I'm probably just going to fall asleep on the recliner watching *Home Alone* or something."

"Are you sure?" I ask, chewing on my lip.

"Of course, kiddo. Get out of here."

"All right." I hop down from the stool, then round the island and press a kiss to his cheek. "Merry Christmas, Uncle Jared."

"Merry Christmas, Em. Tell Mrs. Kelly I said hi, and make sure none of my players break any rules. We have some games to win."

He throws me a playful wink, and I try not to react to the fact that one of his players already has broken a rule...and it's all my fault.

I take a deep breath as I pull into Harper and Collin's neighborhood. On one hand, I'm excited about our little get-together tonight. We don't all get to hang out outside of the rink during the season as much as I'd like.

But on the other hand...spending Christmas with Smith isn't exactly what I had in mind. I know there is no way I'm going to be able to relax tonight knowing he's here. I'm going to have to pretend I don't want to kiss him, pretend I haven't already kissed him.

I breathe a sigh of relief when I pull my little Toyota in behind Hollis' BMW, grateful that Smith isn't here yet.

Thank fuck.

Maybe he canceled? He doesn't usually come to any social gatherings. Not really his scene, which is why I was so surprised when he said he'd be here. Maybe he's bailing and I won't have to endure several hours of pretending around all of our friends. Maybe—

Maybe I'm not that lucky because lights in my rearview mirror grab my attention, and I know it's him.

Fuck.

I close my eyes and smack my head against the headrest a few times, trying to talk myself into just getting out and getting it all over with. *You can do this, Emilia. Just pretend you don't want to rip his clothes off. You got this. You can—*

My thoughts are interrupted by knocking on my window. I don't peel my eyes open because I know who it is.

It's *him*. I can feel his stare.

"Open up, Emilia."

I'm taken back to the nights we spent together with just three simple words, to when I was on my knees for him, his cock pressing against my lips.

"Open up, Emilia."

I drop my jaw.

"Good girl."

I shiver at the memory, wondering if he realizes the effect those words have on me.

He knocks again, and this time I do open my eyes and meet his dark stare that's daring me to continue ignoring him.

I don't.

I push open the door and he's there, grabbing it and holding his hand out for me. I ignore the gesture, pulling myself from the car.

He doesn't miss it.

"I'm surprised you came," I say, alleviating the tension between us.

He shrugs, shoving a hand into his pocket and rocking back on his heels. "Didn't have much else going on, so I figured why not. I used to do Christmas with Bessie and her family, but they're all grown up and out of state, and since Bessie is gone, well…"

He trails off, and it makes me sad for him. Does that mean he's been doing Christmas alone for years? Does that mean he does all holidays alone? I picture him eating takeout on his couch by himself with nobody else around, and there's a dull ache in my chest for him.

"Don't give me that look," he says sharply.

"What look?" I ask innocently.

"Pity." He shakes his head. "I don't need it. Loner, remember?"

I lift my brow. "*Alone*, remember?"

His dark brows slam together, and he looks like he wants to say something but thinks better of it. "I'm here now, aren't I?"

I know that's not what he wanted to say, but I let him have it.

"You are. Bring anything good for the gift exchange?" I ask, trying to peek into the bag in his hand.

He tucks it behind his back, a hint of a smile ghosting his lips. "I'm not telling."

"Oh, come on. It'll be our little secret."

The moment the words leave my lips, I realize my mistake. The air around us changes from playful to serious fast. He lifts his free hand, scrubbing at the scruff covering his face, then sighs.

"Emilia, I—"

"I bring Christmas cheer and Christmas beer!"

Miller's sudden intrusion has us jumping apart. If he notices—which isn't likely because it's Miller—he doesn't say anything.

Smith clears his throat, putting space between us as he slides his free hand into his back pocket.

"Hey, why the long faces? We're here to get lit!"

Smith glares at him. "Do not go in there thinking you're going to get drunk. Hollis and Harper's mother is here."

"Oh shit." His brows rise. "She hot?"

"Miller!"

The guy in question holds his hands up as best he can with a six-pack of beer in each one. "What? It's a genuine question!"

Smith steps toward him, pointing a finger at his face. "Do *not* hit on her, Miller. I mean it."

"Well, if I can't hit on her, who can I hit on?"

"Nobody! Put your dick away."

Miller's shoulders sink and he mutters something that sounds an awful lot like *My dick is always away* as he walks toward the house, but I know that can't be right based on what I've heard about him.

Smith and I follow behind, keeping a respectable distance between the two of us. Miller tries to walk right in, but Smith smacks him across the backside of his head, so he presses the doorbell instead.

It doesn't take long before Collin and Harper are pulling the door open, greeting us with smiles and hugs.

"Beer's here!" Miller shouts, walking into the house.

Collin looks back at us. "Is it too late to uninvite him?"

"Unfortunately, it is. Just watch out for him near your mother-in-law. He's on the prowl."

"Well, hello, *you*," Miller purrs, striding into the kitchen and beelining straight for Hollis and Harper's mom. He bows dramatically, then grabs her hand, placing a kiss on the back of it. "Did my heart love till now?"

"Okay, Shakespeare." Collin charges his way. "You're done."

"Anyone else wildly impressed that Collin knows Shakespeare?" Ryan comments as Miller takes off and Collin chases after him.

"I'm more impressed that Miller knows it," her husband adds, slipping an arm around her waist and tugging her close.

"Either way, I'm flattered," Evelyn, Hollis and Harper's mother, says as she makes her way over to me and pulls me in for a hug. "So good to see you again, Emilia."

I squeeze her tightly, loving the familiar warmth she brings me. Much like Smith's, my childhood isn't much to write home about. My father spent most of his time working and very little time caring about anything I did. My mother tried her best to make up for him but didn't do much to hide the fact that the wine made her smile more than he ever could. If I wasn't at my uncle's, I was spending time at the Kelly household. Evelyn always had a way of making me feel special.

"Hey, Evelyn. You excited about being a grandmother?"

"Very much so. Just wish they'd let it spill what they're having." She looks pointedly at Lowell, who mimics zipping his lips. "So rude." She rolls her eyes playfully, then looks at Smith. "I don't think I've met your boyfriend yet."

The squeak that leaves me is embarrassingly loud, and everyone in the room who knows who Smith is laughs.

"They aren't dating, Mom. That's Smith—he's a teammate of Lowell's," Hollis tells her.

"Hmm…" Evelyn says, her watchful eyes bouncing between the two of us. I don't know what it is she's thinking right now, but based on the way she's studying us so closely, I know I don't like it. "Well, then, Mr. Smith…" She holds her hand out to grasp his. "Nice to meet you."

"It's nice to meet you, Mrs. Kelly. I've heard wonderful things about you from Lowell." He nods toward where Miller and Collin ran off to. "I'm going to go find my moronic teammate who I am very sorry about. He's young. And dumb. Really, *really* dumb."

Evelyn laughs, waving him off. "Please. He's fine. It makes an old lady like me feel good."

He grins at her, then disappears toward the pleas of help that are definitely coming from Miller.

The moment he's out of earshot, she turns to me. "You two truly aren't dating? Because that man is...*wow.*"

"I—no!" I laugh lightly, hoping it sounds convincing enough. "He's just...a player."

She hums again, and I still don't like the reaction. "Interesting."

And I *really* don't like that one.

"Well, never mind," she says, linking her arm in mine. "Come sit next to me. Lowell was just telling us all how he and Hollis met."

Hollis groans, and we all laugh, knowing the story already. Lowell dives back in where he left off, and by the time he's finished, dinner is ready.

We pile into the dining room, and I can't help but laugh at how detailed Harper got with everything. Sitting on each plate is a little Santa-shaped name tag. I guess given her career that utilizes her insanely amazing artistic abilities, I'm not surprised she got all crafty with this.

I find my name and go to pull my chair out, but it's already being done for me. I glance up to see Smith.

"For you," he says quietly.

"Thank you," I murmur back.

Then, even though his name isn't on the card, he takes the seat next to me and reaches over to switch his and Miller's Santa nameplates. When he turns back to me, I lift my brow at him.

"What?" he says innocently. "I saved you. You're welcome."

I sputter out a laugh because he's not wrong.

Miller waltzes into the room and pulls his chair out next to Smith. He takes a seat, then turns to the big giant. Looking him square in the eyes, he says, "I just want you to know that if you try to hold my hand, I will let you."

Smith just looks at him. "Duly noted."

I tuck my lips together, trying not to laugh at the exchange, but it's no use. A small sound escapes me and has Smith turning his heated stare my way, which makes me laugh harder.

"Don't encourage him."

Miller's face pops around Smith's head. "No, please. Encourage me. I like it." He bounces his brows up and down.

If the look Smith gave him before was dark, this one is murderous.

I know then that it's going to be a long night.

CHAPTER 12

Collin and Rhodes are deep in a conversation about the season, and Lowell's pretending he's not listening for any sign of Hollis needing him. Miller is...well, he's lucky he's alive, that's for sure.

I glare over at him. He's been flirting with Emilia all night, and I could wring his neck for it.

I won't lie, it was painful sitting next to her all through dinner. It's easily the longest I've been so close to her in over two years. I had to stop myself no less than three times from reaching out and touching her...holding her hand...kissing her.

But there was no way I was going to let Miller sit next to her. I probably would have killed him. Hell, I still might kill him just for the hell of it.

"I'm grabbing another beer. Does anyone want anything while I'm up?" he announces, rising from the couch.

I jump up after him. "No way you're going in there alone."

"What? Why not?"

"Um, probably because you keep hitting on Mrs. Kelly." *And what's mine—Emilia.* Though I don't say that part aloud.

"Uh, her name is Evelyn," Miller says, rolling his eyes.

It doesn't help his case at all.

"I'm going with you," I say to him.

"Well, I'm going too. I need to check on Hollis." Lowell hops up, jumping ahead of us both.

"Wow." Rhodes shakes his head, then drains the last of his beer. "You're all a bunch of pathetic losers. But I'm out of beer, so I guess I'll go check in with Ryan."

"Yeah, I think I heard Harper call my name for sure." Collin grabs an empty bottle from the table and stands.

It's like they're all in a silent agreement that they miss being near their women, but none of them will fess up to it.

We pad across the house but stop short when Collin holds his hand up, motioning for us to get into formation like we're part of the military or something. I kind of feel like we are as we shamelessly eavesdrop.

"I like him. I really, *really* like him. And he is going to be an amazing father to your baby, Hollis," Evelyn says about Lowell.

Rhodes claps Lowell on the shoulder, grinning at him. The guy smiles less often than I do—and that's really saying something—but we all know how important it was for Lowell to be accepted by Hollis' mom. It's all he's been talking about at the rink for the last week. He's been sweating bullets, but I knew he had no reason to be worried. Lowell is a good guy, and Hollis is lucky to have him as the father of her child.

"Honestly?" she continues. "I'm just glad it's not Thad. That man was a total douchebag. I can still say that, right?"

"Oh my gosh, *thank you!*" Emilia agrees with her, and I can imagine her throwing her hands in the air, her red hair that's always up in a damn ponytail holder bouncing around with the movement. "I have been saying that for *years!* He gave me such bad vibes."

"He really did. He reminded me of your father, actually," Evelyn tells her daughter.

"I had no idea that was what you thought about him, Mom," Hollis says.

"I didn't want to say anything because I knew how much you loved him, and you seemed happy. I thought maybe it was just my own insecurities about my marriage falling apart, and I didn't think it would be fair to put that on your relationship. In the end, it turned out I was right, and that's the last thing I ever wanted. I know you girls think I'm overprotective and all I want to do is smother you, and while that may be partially true, I do it because I love you more than anything and only want what's good for you. I hope you'll understand that soon too. I can tell your man out there with the cute butt does."

I glance over to find his wide eyes glistening under the soft hallway lighting. It's crazy to see how much he's changed since this past summer.

Hell, it's crazy to see how much Collin and Rhodes have changed too, but love does that to you. It turns you into someone else. If you're lucky, it's a good someone else. If you're unlucky…it can do so much more harm than good.

And that's what I'm afraid of—losing everything for a good time that doesn't last. I'm not sure I'm willing to risk it. It's the reason I haven't given myself to anything other than hockey. People let me down. Hockey doesn't, at least not in the same way.

"All right, who is in here talking about my cute butt again?" Collin announces as he rounds the corner.

We follow closely behind him, filing into the kitchen one by one. Emilia's eyes track mine as I grab fresh beers from the fridge, passing them out to the guys. I point to a bottle of wine, silently asking her if she wants another glass. She nods and I pour her one, sliding it her way.

Our fingertips brush around the glass, and while everyone else is too busy to notice the hitch in her breath, I'm not.

I don't miss it because I fucking felt it too.

That charge. That spark.

She downs half the glass in one drink.

"Just because someone mentions a nice butt, doesn't mean they are talking about yours." Harper pats her husband's cheek, pulling our attention.

He snorts. "Right. Sure."

"They could be talking about mine." Miller turns around, jutting his backside out for all to see.

"I can assure you, it was not your ass," Emilia deadpans, glancing down at it anyway.

Yep. He's dying.

"Rude. I think for that, you owe me a present."

Miller glares at her, not noticing that I'm shooting the same fucking look his way, but Emilia sees it, and it's enough to have her throwing back the rest of her drink.

"Is that your way of asking if we can do gifts now?" Harper asks.

He folds his hands under his chin. "Please, Mom?"

She rolls her eyes. "Fine, let's go. Everyone to the big room."

"All right, don't everyone fight over sitting next to me," Miller says, leading the pack. He throws his arm around Emilia, winking at her. "Especially you, gorgeous."

She rolls her eyes but doesn't make a move to push him off. Is she fucking doing this to me on purpose? Does she want me to lose my mind?

We all gather around the tree Harper and Collin have set up in their big, open entertainment room. It's one hundred percent them—a black tree with red lights decked out in horror-themed ornaments. The "star" is Freddy Krueger's knife glove. It would be weird in any other home, but since they're both horror-obsessed, it works.

Miller tugs Emilia down next to him, and she just allows it.

She fucking allows it.

My blood is boiling. I feel so damn stupid for wanting to march over there and stake my claim in front of everyone, for wanting to scream *She's mine.*

But she's *not* mine. Hell, I haven't even kissed her in over two years.

I want to, though. I really fucking want to.

"I'm going to grab more wine," Emilia says, rising from the couch and heading for the kitchen.

Miller juts his bottom lip out, pouting when she walks from the room. "I'll go too."

He tries to follow, and I shove him back down. "Not happening." I scowl at him. "I'll go."

I don't leave any room for him to argue or for anyone to question my motives. I follow behind Emilia and find her in the kitchen, her back to me as she reaches into the fridge for a new bottle of wine. She sets it on the counter but doesn't make a move to open it. Instead, she rests her hands on the countertop and hangs her head.

She looks worn out and tired, and the only thing I want to do is walk over there and make her feel better.

Maybe it's the alcohol making me feel more daring or maybe I'm just an idiot, either way, I cross the kitchen.

I can tell the moment she realizes I'm standing behind her. Her body shifts and she stands up straight, but she doesn't tell me to leave. She doesn't tell me to get away. She just stands there.

Almost like she's waiting.

I shouldn't be doing this. Shouldn't be standing this close to her.

But I can't help it.

I *have* to touch her.

She doesn't stop me when I reach out and fit my hand around her waist. She doesn't stop me when I tug her back against me or when I drop my lips to her exposed neck, not even when I press a kiss there.

A tiny moan escapes her. It's soft, nearly not a noise at all, but I hear it anyway.

Before I can talk myself out of it, I spin her in my arms and lift her, dropping her onto the counter.

"Smith…"

I step between her legs, taking her face in my hands. I slide one hand through her hair, gently tugging the ponytail holder free. Her red curls cascade down her back and over her shoulders.

I lean back to admire her. She looks like a fucking angel sitting there staring up at me with her lips slightly parted and eyes full of lust.

"Fucking perfect."

A small gasp leaves her lips when I repeat the same words to her from our first night together.

"What… What are you doing?"

"Reminding you who you belong to."

Then I crush my mouth to hers. She stills for only a moment before melting into me, and I tug her closer, swallowing the low moan that escapes her and deepening the kiss.

It's heaven. She tastes like heaven. Just like I remember.

No—*better*.

Her lips are soft and sweet and absolutely fucking perfect, just like the way she fits against me is perfect.

I slide my hands through her hair, dragging my fingers through the long, silky strands, and I'm flooded with memories of how good it felt wrapped around my fist as she sank to her knees in front of me.

I pull her closer, her legs going around my waist, and there's no mistaking the evidence of what she's doing to me...or of what I'm doing to her.

Having her against me again...it feels entirely too fucking good. I want to yank her off this counter and carry her to a bedroom and have my way with her.

Hell, I don't even want to do that much. Right here in this kitchen, I want to slide her panties aside and plunge my cock deep inside her, want to see if her pussy still feels like the perfect fit.

I keep one hand wrapped in her hair, the other moving to her thigh, where I slowly slide my hand under her dark green skirt. It's one of the few times I'm glad she's wearing one. I don't waste any time—because I have no idea how long this moment will last—and run the back of my knuckle right over the soaked spot on her panties.

She whimpers against my mouth, her hands clawing at my biceps, trying to get closer. Her body slides against the counter, searching for any sort of friction she can get.

I oblige. I press my knuckle harder against her, finding her clit, and I'm so fucking glad I'm kissing her so I can swallow the loud moan that leaves her.

I'm so wrapped up in her that I nearly miss the footfalls in the hallway.

She doesn't though. She goes stiff in my arms, wrenching her mouth away from me. Her eyes, full of fear, flick to mine. She's on the counter not facing the hall, but I can see over her shoulder.

"Is someone there?" she whispers, too scared to turn around and see for herself.

"No."

And thank fuck too.

We'd be screwed. There's no way we would be able to explain this to someone.

"Oh, thank gosh," Emilia mutters, dropping her head against my chest.

I don't know who was just heading this way, but I'm glad they turned around.

I'm not sure I'm ready for repercussions of this. Which just proves even more that this is a stupid idea.

A stupid idea that feels really, really good.

When my own breathing returns to normal, I tip her

face up to mine, hating how her bottom lip is trapped between her teeth in worry.

"That was…" She swallows, and I already know I'm going to hate her next words. "A mistake," she finishes. "W-We shouldn't have done that."

She's wrong.

She knows she's wrong too. Maybe this wasn't the place, but doing that…it was inevitable.

She shoves at my chest, and I step away, allowing her to slide off the counter. She brushes her hands through her hair, smoothing her clothes back down. She runs the back of her hand across her lips like she's trying to rub away the kiss, but it's no use. Her lips are swollen and used, and she looks every bit like she's been kissed.

"I… We… We can't do that again, Smith."

"I know."

"I mean it."

"I know."

She nods, her lip back between her teeth. "I…okay." Another nod. "All right. I'm…I'm going back out there."

Now it's my turn to nod. "Okay."

She moves past me, and I reach out, wrapping my hand around her wrist to stop her.

"Smith…"

It's not my name, not really. It's a plea. She wants me to let her go, but the truth is, I'm not so sure I can.

And I don't know how to feel about that.

"Wine," I croak out.

"Huh?"

"You came in here for the wine. Don't forget the wine."

"Oh." She marches back past me, grabbing the bottle, then turning back my way. She mutters a quiet "Thanks" as she disappears back to the party.

I don't know if it was for the reminder or the kiss.

All I know is...I am so screwed.

CHAPTER 13

Emilia: I'd like to set up a day where our film crew can follow you around your apartment when you get back.

Emilia: We did this with Woodworth last year, and the fans loved seeing glimpses into his life outside of the rink.

Smith: Well, hello to you too.

Emilia: Sorry. In work mode.

Emilia: Hi.

Smith: This being-followed-around thing...do I have to?

. . .

Emilia: Yes.

Smith: Okay, fine.

Smith: But I'll probably complain about it the entire time.

Emilia: I'll make a note of that.

Smith: Can you also make a note that I'm being forced to do this stupid player profile? I'd like a content warning before every video, please.

Emilia: No.

Emilia: Also, you're extra sassy today. Did someone piss in your cereal?

Smith: I drew the short stick and have to sit next to Miller during travel today.

. . .

Emilia: Wait…do you guys really draw sticks to see who has to sit next to him?

Smith: Yes.

Emilia: OMG!

Emilia: That is so mean!

Smith: You've met Miller, yeah? He's exhausting on a good day.

Emilia: Okay, fine. That's fair.

Emilia: Sorry you have to endure that.

Smith: Trust me, I'm sorry too.

Emilia: Try headphones?

. . .

Smith: Did. They don't work. He keeps talking.

Emilia: Sleeping?

Smith: Also doesn't work. He just talks and talks and talks. Even when I pretend to sleep, he still talks, and I can just FEEL him there, so I can never actually fall asleep.

Emilia: Have you tried kneeing him in the nuts?

Smith: That would be breaking dude code, so no.

Emilia: Protect all nuts, not just your own?

Smith: Are we really discussing my nuts right now?

Emilia: No. We're discussing Miller's.

. . .

Emilia: I'm glad this is on my personal phone and not the company's.

Smith: That wouldn't be awkward at all.

Smith: He's still talking, by the way.

Emilia: What's he even going on about?

Smith: Right now, he's listing the acting credentials for Leonardo DiCaprio.

Smith: Just a few minutes ago he was detailing the timeline of STAR WARS. I have no idea how he's made this jump.

Smith: I'm exhausted and in desperate need of a nap before the game tonight.

Emilia: Go nap so you can win.

. . .

Emilia: Oh, and let me know what day works best for you for the player profile.

Smith: I already told you, none of them.

Emilia: And I already told you, too bad.

Smith: You're about as annoying as Miller.

Emilia: YOU TAKE THAT BACK, OWEN MITCHELL SMITH!

Smith: Cancel the player profile.

Emilia: What's that?? You want to do not one but TWO TikTok dances?

Smith: *glares*

Emilia: Oh no, I'm oh SO terrified.

. . .

Emilia: ^Pure sarcasm, by the way.

Smith: Yeah, I caught that.

Smith: Okay, fine. We can do it the day after I get back since we're off for two days. Happy?

Emilia: About the profile? Yes. About you insulting me? No.

Smith: I apologize that I called Miller annoying. He's like, the HOTTEST guy on the team. Nobody with that great of an ass can be annoying. It's statistically impossible.

Emilia: I'm really not sure you know how statistics work, Miller.

Emilia: Also, looking forward to seeing your black eye during the game tonight.

Smith: What bla

. . .

Smith: Sorry. Clearly Miller stole my phone.

Smith: I'm going to go murder him now.

Emilia: I'll allow it.

Emilia: I was kidding about Miller's black eye, but I'm pleased to see he was in fact sporting a fat lip.

Smith: Little shit stain deserved it too.

Smith: Can you tell me why the guys are sending me memes?

Emilia: Memes?

Smith: Yeah, you know, those funny pictures people make and post on social media.

. . .

Emilia: I know what a damn meme is, Smith. I'm asking you WHAT memes they're sending you.

Smith: Oh.

Smith: Memes of me. During arrival photos.

Emilia: Oh. That.

Smith: Yeah, THAT. You knew?

Emilia: I've...seen some.

Smith: Okay, but WHY are they happening?

Emilia: It kind of went viral in the hockey community. It's all over.

Smith: I'm viral??

. . .

Emilia: Yep. Great exposure for the team. Not so much for you.

Smith: What's so great about the photo?

Emilia: I guess it's because of the intense look in your eyes. You looked like you were ready to murder someone.

Smith: I was.

Smith: The other team, of course.

Emilia: Of course.

Emilia: Also…the comments didn't help the situation.

Smith: THERE ARE COMMENTS?!

Smith: Okay, wow. I just read some of them on the team's Instagram.

· · ·

Emilia: Do you even have an Instagram account??

Emilia: The team is required to follow you if you do.

Smith: I do now, but I don't intend to use it any. I'll probably delete it, especially after reading some of that...stuff.

Smith: Should I respond to them?

Emilia: NO! Never respond to the comments!

Emilia: Actually, don't even read them. Rule number one of the internet is to not even READ the comments. They're dangerous.

Smith: They're...something.

Smith: A lot of people were calling me daddy.

Emilia: It's a compliment.

.   .   .

Emilia: You should have seen the ones we deleted.

Smith: There were MORE???

Emilia: Yes. Some are quite detailed. Reading them was…something.

Smith: All because of a picture??

Emilia: Welcome to the internet, old man.

Smith: *glares*

Smith: I'm not THAT old.

Emilia: Whatever you say, gramps.

Smith: Emilia…

.   .   .

Emilia: Owen…

Smith: You don't do that often.

Smith: Call me Owen, I mean.

Emilia: Oh.

Emilia: You're right. I don't. I guess I never really thought about it.

Emilia: You've been Smith since we met.

Smith: That's fair, I guess.

Emilia: Do you…want me to call you Owen?

Smith: Yes.

Smith: No.

. . .

Smith: I'm not really sure, honestly.

Emilia: I can see that.

Emilia: Is it weird being called by your last name all the time?

Smith: Likely nothing different than what military personnel experience, though sometimes it makes me feel like two different people.

Emilia: Which one is the real you? Smith or Owen?

Smith: Which one do you like better?

Emilia: Some days? Neither.

Emilia: But other days? I like them both.

. . .

Smith: I'll make a note of that.

Emilia: You do that.

Emilia: Good luck tonight.

Smith: Thanks.

Emilia: What are some of your hobbies?

Smith: I don't really have any.

Emilia: None??

Emilia: Puzzles count as a hobby, especially as much as you do it. I already have that listed, so I need a few more, something to build off of for content.

Smith: I don't puzzle anymore.

. . .

Emilia: WHAT? Why not??? You loved it!

Smith: Lost interest.

Emilia: Hmm. That's…sad. You seemed to really use it to help you unwind.

Emilia: You didn't replace it with anything?

Smith: Not really.

Emilia: So what do you do when you're not at the rink?

Smith: Wish I was.

Emilia: Come on. Give me something here.

Smith: I don't know, Emilia. I eat, sleep, and breathe hockey. That's pretty much all I do.

· · ·

Emilia: That can't be ALL. I get that hockey is a full-time job, but there's no way it takes up all of your time.

Smith: Sometimes I volunteer down at the hospital.

Emilia: I know. I cover those.

Smith: No. Outside of the team events.

Emilia: Wait…really???

Smith: Yeah. Keeps me busy.

Emilia: That's… I didn't know that.

Smith: Not really something I do for the accolades, so I don't advertise it.

Emilia: That's really something, Owen.

· · ·

Smith: I'd like to keep that out of the profile if we could.

Emilia: Of course.

Emilia: I'll figure something else out.

Emilia: Thank you.

Smith: You're welcome.

Smith: See you tomorrow?

Emilia: Tomorrow.

CHAPTER 14

EMILIA

"Wow!" Blake whistles, tipping his head back to stare up at the massive building in front of us. "This is...a lot to take in."

We're currently standing outside Smith's apartment building.

The same one I was in two years ago.

The same one where he laid me bare and made me feel like I've never felt before.

And somehow, I have to walk inside and act like I've never been here. Like I didn't fall to my knees in his entryway. Like he didn't take me against his kitchen counter and have me for breakfast. Like I wasn't pressed against the window and fucked from behind for the whole city to see.

And like we didn't just slip up two weeks ago at Christmas.

I have to act like none of that ever happened...all while a film crew is here.

"You know, my best friend, Carsen, grew up wealthy

and Nate and I lived with him in college, but even his place wasn't as grand as this. This is definitely NHL money here."

"Just wait until you see the inside."

The words slip out before I even realize what I've just said.

"You've seen it?" Blake asks, not missing it at all.

"Oh, uh…sort of? Pictures," I lie, and I hate how easily those are beginning to pass from my lips. "I've seen photos from the girls."

"Ah, that makes sense." Blake nods. "Well, come on. Let's get this stuff set up and get started on filming. I'm sure we're losing good lighting or whatever it is film people say."

He leads the way into the building like *he's* the one who has been here before, and I, along with the crew, follow behind.

I'm trying hard to control my breathing as we pile into the elevator.

Being back here is hard.

Being back here after Smith kissed me at Christmas is even harder.

Because now it's not just a memory from two years ago, not when I can still feel his lips on mine.

The guys have been on a six-game road trip, and I've been so happy for the two-week reprieve. Truthfully, I'm scared of seeing Smith again. I almost canceled, but I knew I would have to dodge a million and one questions from Blake on why.

So, here I am, trapped in an elevator with him and three other guys on our camera crew as we make our way to the top floor. The elevator chimes as we arrive, and my heart feels like it's beating a million times a second, like it's going to leap out of my chest and fall on this elevator floor and everybody's going to know what happened between us.

It's ridiculous, I know it is, but I'm nervous.

The doors open and I hold my breath, counting the steps it takes to make it to his door.

Ten.

I count the seconds it takes for him to open it.

Eight.

And I count the seconds it takes for his eyes to meet mine.

Four.

I brace myself…waiting for what, I don't know.

But…nothing happens. There is nothing in Smith's eyes when he looks at me. It's like he didn't just have his tongue in my mouth or have me pinned against a counter where if we hadn't been interrupted, who knows how far it would have gone.

Hell, he hardly looks at me at all.

"Good morning, Mr. Smith!" Blake says cheerfully, clapping his hands together. He's a total morning person, and as seen at the rink, the grumpy hockey player in front of us is not.

Based on the grunt that leaves Smith, I can see that hasn't changed much.

Blake just laughs it off as Smith opens the door wider, letting us all into his expansive apartment. When I walk past, I try to make eye contact, but he refuses to meet my stare.

Frankly, it pisses me off, because seriously…he's blowing me off?!

I shouldn't be upset. I really shouldn't considering the kiss should have never happened, but it stings in a way I wasn't expecting.

"This is an incredible place you have here." Blake spins in a circle, taking in the dwelling I'm familiar with.

"Thanks," Smith says quietly. "It's nothing like you'd get from Wright or Rhodes, but it's all I got."

He's definitely right about that. If we were shooting there, we would see the touches of Ryan and Harper and the lives they're building together. This is clearly a bachelor pad. There's next to no furniture, no real décor. It's all very minimalistic and missing that touch to make it feel like a home.

"Still…" Blake laughs. "It's nicer than any place I'll ever have unless Nate takes up stripping or something and starts raking in the dough." He tips his head, picturing that. "Never mind." He points around the room. "Nobody give him that idea. He's an awful dancer."

We all laugh.

I've met Nate a few times during functions with the team, and it's obvious they're madly in love with each other. Blake told me a bit of their story, how they grew up best friends and didn't realize until college that they were ready to take the next step in their relationship, how things were a little touch and go with them for a while, but they've overcome it. Now, after moving down here from Massachusetts to start fresh, they have a little girl their friend Elliott helped bring into this world, and they're happier than they've ever been.

When he told me the story, I was happy for him. Hell, I'm still happy for him…and maybe a little jealous too.

But now isn't the time to dwell on what I don't have…even if he is in the room with me.

"So, uh, where did you guys need to set up?" asks the man I can't seem to get out of my head.

"Did Emilia run through what we're looking for today?"

Smith's eyes flick to mine for only a moment. "Kind of. Something about my rest-day routine, right?"

"Pretty much, yeah," Blake answers. "She can explain while we start setting up the cameras and finding the best places for some shots for lighting and everything."

He and the camera operators head from the room toward the kitchen to get to work. Hopefully, we can capture enough usable material in the next few hours and won't have to come back here.

Smith looks pained as they go, leaving just the two of us alone together. There's a hushed silence that falls over the room, and I don't know what to say to him. It seems like he doesn't know what to say to me either, so we stand there in uncomfortable silence for far too long.

So long that I can't stand it and I blurt out the first thing that comes to mind. "How was your road trip?"

It's a stupid question, so I'm not surprised when he pins me with a dark stare.

"We lost. A lot."

I nod because I know they did. I read the comments the fans left; they weren't pretty, but I don't tell him that.

This feels awkward being here with him, and I'm not entirely sure why. We texted a few times while he was gone to set up this interview, and everything was cordial. It seemed like maybe we could move past what happened.

But this? Being here in this apartment with him when it holds so many memories? It doesn't seem like we've moved past anything. It's like so many more floodgates have been opened and I'm starting to drown, desperate for land right now.

I clear my throat. "Right. So, uh, for today…we just want to follow you around and see what it is you get up to on a rest day. For some reason, the fans are more curious about that than game days. I think it just kind of makes you more…real to them. Little more normal and less of a hockey superstar."

He snorts. "I'm not a hockey superstar. I'm practically a washed-up old man by now. Most people won't remember my name whenever I leave this league."

My chest aches for him because he sounds so

certain, like he actually believes that, and I can't understand why. Sure, he doesn't have the same numbers as McDavid, Ovechkin, or Crosby, but he's an incredible player in his own right. I just wish he'd see that.

Now isn't the time for me to stroke his ego, though. It's time for work, and that's what we're going to do.

"Okay, well, let's start with meals since it's always a question that gets asked. Show us what you can do in the kitchen."

For the first time since I stepped foot in his apartment, he looks at me for more than two seconds. With the one look, I know exactly what's going through his mind, because the last time I was here, he definitely showed me what he can do in the kitchen…and I was his meal.

Ignoring his heated expression, I spin on my heel, only to come to a complete stop. Hanging above the fireplace isn't a TV like you'd normally see in someone's house.

No.

It's our puzzle. The one we left unfinished on the table when our clothes became a distraction.

He kept it.

I stare up at the castle, the same one I told him I wanted to see one day as I regaled him with plans of a trip to Europe I'm almost certain I'll never get to take. I'm lost in the landscape, taken back to a time when I wasn't worried about who he is, just how he made me feel. If it wasn't for the warmth that spreads through me, I wouldn't notice when he steps up behind me.

He's standing so close I can *feel* him, even though he's not touching me.

"There were a lot of things about that weekend left unfinished, but I couldn't bear to leave that the same way," he says in a low, deep voice, his lips nearly brushing my ear.

Then he steps away from and around me. This time, it's his turn to walk away.

"How's my baby doing?"

Hollis' laughter fills my car. "You always have to ask about my baby first, huh?"

"Well, yeah, have to make sure my little angel is doing okay."

"You say angel, I say demon."

"Uh-oh." I frown at the exhaustion laced in her words. "Still having morning sickness?"

"Oh yeah. You do not want to know how many times I've thrown up today."

She's been struggling with it throughout the entire pregnancy, and I hate it for her.

"But enough about me and my struggles," she says. "I was just calling to see how you are. I know I just saw you at Christmas, but it feels like it's been forever."

To say Tori has been on my ass about getting the

player profile started would be an understatement. I tried to explain to her that I'm trying to respect their game schedule *and* Smith's personal time, but she wasn't having any of it. Part of me wonders if she can see through that and can tell that, especially since Christmas, I really don't want to spend time with Smith. I don't trust myself around him. A few minutes alone in the kitchen on Christmas Day proved that to be a valid concern.

"I'm sorry," I tell Hollis. "I promise to be back to begging *you* to hang out soon—if you have time for me, that is. You know, when you're not bumping uglies with your baby daddy."

She groans at my words, but I still hear the smile in the sound. Things with her and Lowell seem to be going okay after Christmas, and I'm happy for them. Lowell has always been a great guy.

"Speaking of hot hockey players…how's it going with Smith? Who, by the way, I still can't believe agreed to do the profile," Hollis says. "He's even more private than Lowell, and that's saying something."

I laugh because she's right. After working with Lowell for the last couple of years, it's safe to say he is indeed private. Hell, I think only about five of his teammates have ever even been to his house. Any time he has his captain's duties and has to host a dinner or something, he either has it at a restaurant or rents an Airbnb.

He's probably one of the nicest guys you'll ever meet and he'd do anything to help a friend, but emotionally? That man is a brick wall. I've heard whispers that it's because of a past relationship gone bad, but I've never dug deeper into it.

"Things with Smith are..." *Complicated. Weird. Tense. Electric.* "They're fine."

"Just fine?" she presses, and guilt nibbles at me. Hollis still has no clue about our history, and right now, when she's already stressed to the max about having a baby with her one-night stand, I'd rather not throw all the sordid details at her.

Besides, nobody can know. I have a promotion to protect.

"Yep. Blake and I actually just wrapped up shooting some content at his apartment. It took way longer than I wanted, but oh well."

We planned to be in and out by lunch, but after some battery issues and other things that came up, we got started late. It's nearly five now, and I'm just heading home.

"Hmm..."

"What are you *hmm*-ing me for?"

"Nothing. It's just..." She trails off, then sighs. "I don't know. I thought there might be something between you two. You disappeared at Christmas together, and then when you came back, your hair was down, and you left rather quickly after that."

"We were just talking, and I wanted to get out of there before I started drinking too much, which was where I was headed dealing with Miller's advances. Just being safe." *Lies, lies, lies.* "Besides, there are rules against staff and players having relationships, you know."

I don't know if I'm reminding her or myself.

"Yeah, but who has to know, right?" She laughs.

I laugh too, hoping it doesn't sound too forced.

Because...she kind of has a point. Who has to know, right?

No, no, no. Stop that, Emilia. Don't even go there.

"Only kidding," she says, pulling me back to the conversation. "Well, kind of. *Oof.*"

"Everything okay?" I ask.

"Ugh. Yeah, just gassy. Pregnancy farts are a bitch."

"Yeah, no thanks on that."

"Trust me, never get knocked up. You'll regret it."

But even as she says the words, I know she's lying. She might hate being pregnant sometimes, but she is already madly in love with her baby, and I really can't wait to watch that love grow once the baby is here.

"We're still planning the baby shower for All-Star weekend, right? You requested off?" she asks.

"Yep. Blake's taking care of everything, so I'm all yours."

"Yay! I'll—" I hear a faint knock through the speaker. "Oh crap, my dinner is here. Hang on."

She grunts, and I can imagine her pulling herself with her swollen belly off the couch. I listen as she unlatches the door, then pulls it open.

"Special *dick*livery for one hot piece of ass."

I can't help it—I burst out laughing as Lowell's words filter through the speaker.

"Oh my gosh," Hollis mutters. "You think it sounds bad, but it's worse—he just humped the air."

"Are you sure that's not Miller?"

"Are you on speaker? Is that Emilia?" The mortification is clear in his voice. "Fuck," he curses, and I laugh again. "Pretend you didn't hear that, Emilia, and I'll do whatever TikTok video you want me to!"

"*Any?*" I ask, my mind already spinning.

"Within reason."

"It's a deal," I say. "Hollis, I love you, but I don't want to be here while you get your *dick*livery, so I'm going to go."

"Bye! I love you!" she says.

Before I can press end, I hear, "Come here, darlin'. I get to eat first."

Her squeal is cut off when the call ends, and I'm thankful for it.

And maybe a little jealous.

I wish I could have something that easy. Well, their situation isn't exactly easy, but still. At least she can have what she wants. Me? I'm stuck wanting what I can't have.

Another call comes in, and I press the green button.

"Oh, thank gosh!" Blake's panicked voice comes over the speaker before I even have a chance to greet him.

"Everything okay?"

"Yes—well, no. Listen, don't hate me, but..." He hesitates. "I kind of left the laptop with all the footage on it at Smith's, and I have dinner reservations with Nate and our surrogate and her husband tonight."

I groan. "And you need me to go get it because those files need to be sent to editing ASAP."

He sucks air in through his teeth. "Yeah, that."

"I think I might murder you, Blake."

"Well, that's rude."

"Is it though?"

"Incredibly. But also a little justified." He pauses. "Is there any way you can do me a solid? I'll owe you. Big time."

"It's fine. You're already covering All-Star weekend for me. I can grab the laptop and get the stuff sent over. We'll be square?"

"Really?" He lets out a relieved sigh. "Thank you. So much. You're the best."

"Yeah, yeah, I know. Have a good dinner."

"Kisses!" He blows them through the phone, and I end the call.

I was almost home, almost to a glass of wine I so desperately need. Instead, I whip a U-turn and make my way back to Smith's apartment.

After sitting in traffic for far too long, I'm officially annoyed. I could wring Blake's neck for this. But then again, it's not like I had any plans tonight. I was just going to order Chinese and sip my way through a whole bottle of wine. Now, I think I'll skip the wine and just eat ice cream for dinner in the bathtub.

When I pull up to his building, it seems even bigger

than it did just a little bit ago. Darker. More intimidating. I chalk it up to coming back here alone.

In and out. Just grab the laptop and leave, Emilia.

I swallow down my nerves and climb out of the car. I do every breathing exercise I can possibly remember as the elevator takes me back to the top floor and my feet carry me to his door.

I knock.

Then wait.

There's a shuffle from the other side, and when he pulls the door open, his head tips to the side.

"Emilia."

"Smith."

We don't say anything else.

We just stand there for several seconds, eyes locked, neither of us moving, neither of us breathing.

One.

Two.

Three.

Four.

Five.

"Do you want to come in?"

I should say no.

I *know* that. It's right there on the tip of my tongue.

But it's not what comes out at all.

"Okay."

And I walk over the threshold.

CHAPTER 15

I'll be honest, I wasn't completely surprised to see Emilia when I pulled my door open. I spotted the laptop on my countertop not long after they left...and I admittedly prayed it would be her who came back for it.

It looks like my prayers were answered.

She steps into my apartment, the door making a hushed *snick* as I close it behind her. She hesitates for only a moment in the foyer before carrying herself farther into the living room, shoulders pressed back like she's trying to will some confidence into herself. Her red hair is still swept up into a messy bun, and I have the urge to reach over and pull it free, let it tumble down her back the way I like it.

Her steps falter in the middle of the room, eyes going to the puzzle hanging over the fireplace.

I meant what I said to her earlier about it. When I walked back into my apartment all alone on the night she left, that puzzle was sitting on the table taunting me. I didn't touch it though. I couldn't for some reason. It didn't feel right to just get rid of something we'd done together. It felt like I was trying to get rid of her when all I wanted to do was hold on for dear life.

So, it sat there for *months* unfinished and untouched. My housekeepers were thoroughly annoyed with me, but I didn't care. I just let it collect dust and soak in all the memories of our weekend together.

Then, we went back to the rink for preseason, and I was introduced to the team's newest social media manager.

Her.

That night when I got home, I almost threw it away. I had the trash can there, ready to scoop the pieces inside and never look at it again.

But I couldn't.

So, I finished it. Stayed up way too fucking late doing it and was nearly late to practice the next day, but I completed it.

It's been hanging in that same spot since. Maybe I'm an idiot for keeping it and being constantly reminded of what happened between us, but I don't regret it— especially not seeing the look on her face now.

"Would you like something to drink?" I ask, and she jumps at my words.

"Oh…uh…" She gives herself a shake. "I, uh, I'm here for a laptop. Blake forgot to grab it. If I can get it, then I'll just be on my way."

I lift a brow, amused by how she's stumbling over her words and how she's not even looking at me.

She's nervous.

I like that she's nervous.

I step into her, tucking a knuckle under her chin and tipping her head up until her eyes meet mine. "Have a drink with me, Emilia."

"Okay."

She says it so easily I'm not even sure she remembered to pretend to resist. I don't give her time to realize though, pulling the jacket from her shoulders and tossing it onto the couch before making my way to the kitchen.

I try not to think about how I shouldn't be doing this. How I should just hand her the laptop and send her on her way. How I shouldn't be tempting fate more than I already am.

But it's one drink. There's no harm in that, right?

I work fast, grabbing a glass from the cabinet and pouring her wine, then making my way back out to the living room. She's still standing in the same spot, staring up at the castle. I hand her the wine, noting the way the liquid shakes as she takes a healthy drink. I do the same, keeping my eyes on hers.

"Did you go?" I ask. She raises her brows, and I nod toward the picture. "The trip you wanted to take to Europe, the one you had all planned—did you make it happen?"

She laughs quietly. "No. I got wrapped up in work."

I frown, remembering how excited she was, how badly she wanted it, how detailed her plans were. I hate that she never went. I hate that she never got to experience everything she wanted.

I'll take you.

The words bounce around in my head, but I don't say them even though I mean every single one…and I don't know how to feel about that. I don't know how to feel about the fact that if I didn't have a game coming up, I'd put our asses on a plane right now and we'd go anywhere she wanted to go.

I shouldn't want any of that. I have no right to it.

But I do.

She sighs. "Maybe one of these days I can do it. After I get the director job possibly? A celebration trip of sorts."

Even as she says it, I can tell she knows she's lying to herself. She won't take that vacation on her own. She'll work herself to death first, and while that makes me sad, I understand it. I've dedicated my entire life to hockey, so I have no room to talk or judge.

"Yeah, maybe," I mutter, taking a sip of my whiskey.

"What about you? What's the biggest or best trip you've ever been on?"

"This one."

She tips her head. "This one?"

"Well, being from Canada, yeah, I consider this whole NHL thing one big trip."

"NHL thing," she mutters, shaking her head and taking another sip of her wine. "That's an interesting way to describe over fifteen years in the league."

I try not to think too hard about that reality, about how long I've been playing. All it does is remind me that pretty soon, this will all be gone, and I'll truly be alone.

"Uh-oh. Did I say something wrong?"

"Hmm?" I pull myself from my morbid thoughts, looking over at her. Her brows are pinched together in concern. I shake my head. "No, it's nothing. Just…thinking."

"About retiring?"

My head snaps back. "We don't say the R-word."

"My bad." She laughs softly. "Is that what you're thinking about though?"

It's no secret that my contract with the Comets is up this year, just like the fact that I'm getting up there in age isn't a secret. Everyone knows after this season, there's a real possibility of me never playing again.

"You could say it's been on my mind." I run my hand over my beard. "Is that why you wanted me for the player profile? Because this could be my last year?"

"It was entirely decided by fan votes," she says. "I promise that's the only reason."

I nod, believing her.

I wondered if this was some sort of pity thing from the team, like a *Hey, thanks for giving us your all for your entire career. You're still getting the boot at the end of the season, but how about we make you feel just a little bit special first* type of deal.

I guess it's really not though.

I down the rest of my whiskey, then hold the empty glass up to her in a silent question. She looks down at her still half-full glass of wine, shrugs, and finishes it in one gulp.

I lead the way to the kitchen, where I set to work refilling both of our drinks.

"Can I ask you something totally off the record?"

"Anything," I say over my shoulder.

"*Is* this your last year?"

I swallow. I had a feeling that was what she was going to ask, but it's the one question I can't really answer.

I go with something neutral. "It's not really up to me, is it?"

"No. I guess it's not," she says quietly as I pass her a fresh glass of wine. She rolls her lips together, like she is considering asking me something else but is unsure if she can.

"Whatever it is that's going through your head, just ask." I stand opposite her, back pressed against the counter. "I'm an open book."

She laughs and takes a sip of her wine, then sets it aside. "People have called you many things over the years, Smith, but they've never called you an open book."

"With you I am."

Her laughter fades quickly, and she looks to the side, a faraway gaze in her eyes. I wonder if she's remembering our weekend together too, how we shared so much with one another without sharing any of the basics. Somehow, leaving out those details, it meant more. Where we work, our names, where we live…those are just things about us. They don't *make* us. Our dreams, how we fill our downtime, the things we yearn for...those make us.

That weekend we spent together, that's exactly what we shared—our real selves with zero expectations and zero preconceived notions.

She clears her throat. "Do you *want* to keep playing?"

In all my years of being in the NHL, I don't think anyone has ever asked me that before...not even me. It's a question I've been scared to ask because I'm scared of the answer.

Do I want to keep playing? There's a huge part of me that's screaming, *Yes! Of course!* But there's also that lonely part of me...the one that's pushed aside *everything* for hockey...that says no, says it's time to hang up my skates and move on.

"I don't know," I answer honestly. "Some days I wake up and crave the game. Others, I wake up and crave something else...something...*more.*"

She nods like she understands, though I'm not sure she does because I don't even understand.

I can't imagine not playing hockey, but I can't imagine doing anything else either.

Hell, do I even have the skills to do anything else? Hockey is all I've ever known, and I have no idea what I'm going to do whenever I am actually done with the game.

"Owen?" I drag my gaze to hers. She's peering up at me, the green of her eyes catching the setting sun just right as it filters through the big, open windows that make up the west side of my apartment. "You're allowed to want other things."

"Am I?"

"Of course." She gives me a lopsided smile. "You can have whatever you want."

There's a charge in the room, and the energy shifts as her words settle around us.

I can't have whatever I want. She knows that as well as I do.

Her smile falters when I push off the counter and take a step her way. "O-Owen…"

I take another step closer to her, even though I know I shouldn't. I should be putting distance between us, not closing it, but I can't stop myself.

"Not you, huh, Emilia?" She swallows when I take another step. "I can't have you."

Her tongue slides across her lips, her breaths coming in sharper as I get closer to her.

She doesn't make a move to stop me, so I don't. I don't stop until I'm standing mere inches away, until I can feel her chest brushing against me with every heavy breath she draws in and pushes out. Her green eyes are glassy and filled with so many questions, but even more than that, they're filled with desire.

She wants this as badly as I do.

With one hand on her waist, I use the other to tug the clip that's holding her hair up free, watching as her gorgeous red waves tumble down.

"You should wear your hair down more often."

She nods, looking up at me like she'd do anything I asked her to.

I like that. I like having her at my mercy, like her desire to please me.

I slip my fingers through her hair, letting the strands tangle around my fist. I tug her closer, her lips parting on a small gasp. She's practically panting now, and I love it because I haven't even done anything yet, haven't even really touched her.

But I want to.

I really, *really* fucking want to.

I know if we cross that line, though, there's no going back. There's no stopping. If we start this, we're finishing it.

I can't walk away. Not again.

I need her to realize that too.

"Is this what you want?"

She nods.

"What did I tell you before?"

Her brows tighten for only a moment before her eyes spark with the memory. "My words. Use my words."

"Good girl."

I *feel* her knees buckle when I say it, and I catch her, lifting her up and setting her on the countertop. I step between her legs, loving the way I fit there.

"Is this what you want?" I repeat, fingers still tangled in her hair.

"Yes."

It's the single greatest word I've ever heard.

"Thank fuck," I mutter, barely getting the words out before sealing my mouth against hers.

She moans the moment our lips touch, and I swallow the sound. I tug on her hair, tipping her head back to get just the right angle as our tongues brush. I slide my hands from her hair and down her sides, tugging her shirt free from that same fucking skirt that has starred in far too many of my fantasies.

I break our kiss only to tug the simple navy-blue blouse over her head, loving the way her red hair spills down her back as she sits there in just her lacy black bra, her tits—which I know fit into my hands perfectly—threatening to spill over the cups.

I admire her for only a beat, then reach behind her and undo her bra, slipping the material down her arms and chucking it across the kitchen. I have no clue where it lands, and I don't care.

All I care about is getting my mouth on her tits.

Fuck she looks like an angel sitting there, and I'd be a damn liar if I said I didn't want to do bad, bad things to her. I bury my face against her chest, and she groans when I close my mouth around her nipple, sucking on the rosy bud with fervor, her hands crashing into my hair, holding me close.

I spend so long sucking on her tits that her groans turn into little whimpers, and I know she wants more.

I want more too.

I wrench my shirt off over my head, then drop my fingers to the button on my pants and unsnap them, lifting her off the counter and setting her on her feet. I unzip her skirt, letting it pool at her feet.

"Leave them on," I say as she goes to toe her heels off.

She looks up at me, almost looking like she wants to argue but thinks better of it. Instead, she steps free of her skirt, leaving the black pumps in place, standing before me in nothing but them and a black lace thong. Her chest is red from my beard scratching against her, and it's heaving up and down. She looks gorgeous.

But she'd look even better on her knees.

"Do you remember what we did before?" I ask. Her nostrils flare, and she nods. "Good. Get on your knees and take my cock out, Emilia."

She drops to the floor, her hands flying to my jeans.

The sound of the zipper running along the track is loud, but not as loud as the sharp breath she sucks in when she tugs my jeans and underwear down, my dick finally springing free.

I don't even have to tell her to drop her jaw, and I fucking love that. She flattens her tongue, eager for me to fill her mouth, to use her.

So, I do.

I wrap her hair around my fist, and I slide my cock into her warmth, loving the guttural moan that leaves her, loving the way she sucks me back, like she's been waiting for this moment forever. Slowly, I push my cock to the back of her throat until I'm as far in as she can take me.

"Look at me," I tell her, tugging her hair. I use my other hand to stroke my thumb over her jaw, helping her relax as I try to push in just a little more.

Her eyes are glassy, and her face is turning just the lightest shade of red. It's the most beautiful sight I've ever seen.

"You're doing such a good job," I say. "Just perfect."

Any tension she was holding melts away, and I'm able to work my cock in just a few more centimeters before pulling out entirely. She gasps for air, and I let her take it in.

Then, I do it again. Over and over she swallows my cock, taking more and more each time. I can feel my orgasm lurking, and I don't want to come in her mouth. Not this time.

I tug her to her feet, kissing her hard before spinning her around and laying her face-first on the counter.

"Grip the other side," I tell her, and she listens without hesitation.

I kick her feet apart and stand back. I don't need to slip my fingers between her legs to know she's wet. I can see her arousal shining on the inside of her thighs. But I do it anyway, pulling her thong to the side and plunging two fingers inside of her.

"*Fuck!*" she cries out, bucking off the counter at the sudden intrusion. "Oh god."

I can't help but chuckle at the sounds leaving her, desperate and needy and so fucking hot.

"Please, please, please," she chants.

"Please what, Emilia?" I twist my fingers, rubbing against that elusive spot I know drives her wild. "What do you want?"

"You!" she begs. "I want you!"

I reach into my back pocket with one hand and pluck my wallet free. I grab the condom I had the forethought to put in there and rip the wrapper open with my teeth, sheathing myself with one hand before pulling my fingers from her greedy cunt.

She whimpers at the loss, but soon her cries turn into pleasured moans as I sink into her. My pace is leisurely, a stark contrast to the way I was fucking her with my fingers. I slowly work my cock in, letting her adjust to my size.

When I'm fully seated, I have to take a breather. I'm so close to coming just from the sheer relief of being inside her again.

Being with her feels like coming home. It feels *right*.

"Please, Owen. *Move*."

I'm more inclined to give directions rather than take them, but I can't find it in me to argue with her request. So, I fuck her slowly—almost painfully so. I don't know how long this is going to be mine, so I'm going to savor it.

She holds on to the counter tightly, pushing back to meet my thrusts, letting me worship her at my leisure. I have no idea how long I do it. It feels like seconds and minutes and hours. Somehow, it's still not long enough. It will never be long enough, because being inside of her will never get old.

My balls tighten, and I know I'm getting close. If the way her breaths are getting sharper and shorter is any indication, I know Emilia is too.

I can't hold back any longer—I slide my hand around her, pressing fingers against her clit as I slam into her.

"Yes! God, yes!"

"Wrong name, sweetheart," I say, slamming into her again.

Even with her heels still on, she's on her tiptoes, pushing back to meet my hard thrusts. I rub tight circles on her clit, pumping my cock in and out of her, and it's not long before I feel her legs shake, her pussy clenching around me as she falls apart.

She goes limp on the counter, but I don't stop pounding into her, chasing my own release. Not even a minute later, I find it, emptying myself into the condom, wishing it was her.

I slow my thrusts as I come down from the high, running my hands over her back, soothing her as she catches her breath. Then I gather her in my arms, spinning her around and lifting her. She hooks her legs around my waist, resting her head on my shoulder as I press kisses to her temple.

"You did so good, Emilia."

She makes a contented sound as I carry her through the apartment to my bathroom. I set her down on the bench in the walk-in shower, drag her underwear down her legs, strip her heels from her feet, then get rid of the condom. I turn the water on, letting it warm up, then pull her to her feet and begin washing her hair.

We alternate between kissing and cleaning, but we don't speak. When we're finished, I wrap her in a towel, then carry her to the bed. I bury us beneath the covers, tugging her close to me until she's practically lying on top of me.

Sleep has nearly claimed me when our silence is finally broken.

"Owen?" she says in the darkness of the room.

"Hmm?"

"Thank you."

"Thank *you*."

"You're welcome."

I chuckle, then press a kiss to her head. "Sleep, Emilia. You're going to need it."

She laughs softly, and I swear I hear her say, "I can't wait."

CHAPTER 16

EMILIA

I'm on fire.

At least I *feel* like I'm on fire. There's sweat coating the back of my neck, and I feel like my body is running at least ten degrees hotter than normal.

And it's all because of Smith.

I'm plastered to his side, my head resting on his chest, and his arm is holding me in place against him. I've been lying here for the last thirty minutes running my hand through the hair on his torso, waiting for him to wake up, waiting to see how he feels about last night.

I should feel a crushing weight of guilt right now. I'm sure somewhere buried deep inside the dark crevices of my mind, it's just sitting there waiting and ready to show its true weight—but in this moment, I don't feel anything other than pure bliss.

This is everything that's been missing. Last night, it felt like I was snapped back into reality.

I try not to think about the fact that I put my career

in jeopardy last night. If anyone were to find out about this...I'd be toast. Totally screwed. I—

Smith stirs under my palm, and I hold my breath, waiting for him to finally wake up. I'm dying to know what he's thinking. The rule of no relationships doesn't just apply to me. It's on him too.

But nothing happens. He doesn't move.

I sigh. He laughs.

I gasp, trying to push up, but he tightens his hold, dragging me until I'm all the way on top of him.

"You're awake!" I glare down at him.

His body rumbles with laughter. "I've been awake."

"For how long?"

"Just a few minutes." He dances his fingertips over my temple. "Your loud thinking woke me up."

I nibble on my bottom lip. "Sorry. It's just...I'm having thoughts."

"About last night?"

I nod. "Yes."

"That's understandable." He rubs his thumbs into the small of my back, and I hear him swallow. "Do you regret it?"

"No!"

And it's the truth. I don't regret last night. It was everything I could have hoped for.

But that doesn't mean it was right.

"I don't regret it," I say. "It's just..." I blow out a breath. "What the hell are we doing, Smith?"

His dark brows furrow, and I'm not sure if it's my question that does it or if it's me calling him Smith again.

I push off his chest, and this time he lets me move. I straddle him, trying hard to ignore the way his dick stirs to life against my ass.

"I have a promotion. You have a contract. We know the rules. We—"

Smith presses his finger against my lips, cutting my words off. I pinch my brows together in question.

"Do you remember that bubble we had before?" I nod, because of course I do. I hated leaving it, but I had to. "Let's make a new one."

"What do you mean?"

"I mean, when we're here together, it's just us having a good time. That's it. Nothing else."

"But—"

He presses his finger harder against my lips, shaking his head, and I roll my lips in. He curls his hand over my waist, sliding it up my back and pulling me down until I'm lying on his chest again, our mouths just inches apart.

"We already know all the reasons it's wrong, Emilia," he says, brushing his nose against mine. "So, let's focus on all the reasons it's right."

"Like?"

"Like the way you take my cock, for one."

"Yes."

The word slips free, and he chuckles, his laughter vibrating through my whole body.

I don't know if I'm agreeing with him or asking him for it. Either way, he lifts his hips, and said cock slips between my ass cheeks. I press back, searching—no, *yearning*—for more.

I've never explored anal play before—my ex wasn't into it—but feeling Smith back there…it feels good, and judging by the way his eyes flare when I press back, he agrees.

I do it again, and his eyes darken.

"Is that what you want, Emilia? For me to play with your ass?"

A blush creeps up my cheeks, and I nod.

"Do you trust me?" he asks.

"Yes." My answer is automatic, and it's honest. I know he'd never do anything to hurt me.

"Good. Turn around. On your stomach."

I do as he instructs, lying facedown. He straddles my legs, tracing his hands over my back, then lower. His hands knead my cheeks, spreading me and massaging me slowly, thumbs circling closer and closer to my untouched hole with each pass.

I shiver at the anticipation, and he doesn't miss it, leaning forward to pepper kisses across my back. His lips never leave me as he makes his way lower, kissing every inch of my ass, continuing to massage me.

"Has anyone ever fucked you back here?" he asks.

"N-No," I admit. "Nothing."

He growls his approval, spreading me wider. "Good. Because I want it first."

I should be completely embarrassed by the pleasure-filled noise that leaves me at the idea of him slipping into me where nobody else has ever been, but I can't find an iota of a fuck to give.

I want it. I want him to have every part of me.

I let out a loud yelp when I feel something wet against my hole, and then it hits me what it is—his tongue.

Oh god. Smith has his tongue on my asshole, and I love it. He rolls it against me, kissing me in a spot I never in a million years imagined I'd allow someone to go, and it feels incredible.

I have no idea how long he licks at me, but it's enough to have me squirming and needing more.

"You're incredible," he says, pulling away, and I already miss his mouth on me. "Just incredible."

He continues to massage my ass as he leans away, reaching into his bedside drawer, and I have a feeling I already know what he's grabbing. There's a hushed *click* as he flips open the lid to the lube. I try to calm my racing heart, nervous I'm not going to like it or it's going to hurt.

I jump a little when I feel the blunt tip of his finger against my hole.

"Relax," he says, rubbing my cheeks but leaving his finger there. I do my best to listen, sucking in small, steady breaths. "Good girl."

The two simple words have me melting like a puddle of goo, and I had no idea I needed to hear them as badly as I do. He takes the chance to slip the tip of his finger in. It feels…strange, but good.

"You okay?"

I nod.

"Words, Emilia," he reminds me.

"Y-Yes. I'm okay. I want…more."

He obliges, pushing the digit in farther, working it in and out over and over again. The small bite of pain goes away, and before I know it, my hips are moving on their own, seeking more of his touch.

He wraps his arm around my middle, pulling me up to my knees. I cry out when the angle changes, sending him deeper. I *need* him deeper.

I need… "More."

He chuckles darkly, then pulls away completely. I'm about to protest, but then I feel more lube drip onto me followed by the obvious intrusion of not one but two fingers pressing against my hole.

"Relax for me, sweetheart. I got you."

And I do.

Slowly, he works two fingers inside, mimicking the same thing he did before, and it's not long before I'm pushing back, seeking his thrusts.

"Jesus, you're killing me," he mutters. "So damn beautiful."

I'm killing him?! He's killing *me*! Having him in my ass…it's so good. Almost too good. The noises leaving my mouth…they're scandalous. I should be mortified at the way I'm arching back into him, begging him for more.

Because I *need* more. I need something.

I reach a hand between my legs, and just as my fingertips graze my clit, he's there, grabbing my hand and trapping it behind my back so I can't touch myself.

"Smith!"

"Not yet." Another dark laugh fades into a groan. "Fuck. Your ass is going to look so pretty taking my cock."

I groan. "Y-Yes. *Please.*"

"Soon. Not today. I need time to stretch you more, and right now, I don't have that patience." He withdraws his fingers, and I cry out at the loss. "Don't move."

I don't dare.

I hear him back inside the bedside table, then the telltale sounds of a condom being ripped open and rolled on.

"I need to be in you," he mutters, and that's all the warning I get before he's thrusting into me *hard*.

"Oh *fuck*!" I scream out, my pussy clenching around him, pulling him in deep and begging for more.

He gives it to me. He gives it *all* to me. His hips slam into me so hard I know at this time tomorrow, I'm still going to be able to feel him, and I can't wait for it.

"Mine," he grunts, pounding into me. "Your pussy is mine."

Yours. Yours. Yours.

"And one day, this ass will be mine too."

He slides his fingers back into my ass, and the sensation of being filled in both holes is almost too much. I feel stuffed and used, but in the best kind of way. There's sweat dripping down my neck, and my breaths are so sharp my chest is literally aching. My arms hurt from being pinned back, and I just feel so...*done*.

"Fuck, you take me so good, Emilia. So damn good."

"Please, Owen. *Please*," I beg, but I don't know what I'm begging for. More? For him to stop? For a release?

Being him, he knows exactly what I need. He lets go of my wrist, and I sigh at the relief.

"Touch yourself."

I heed his instruction, slipping my hand between my legs, drawing *one, two, three* short circles on my clit before I cease to exist on this planet. Everything goes blissfully quiet as my orgasm races through me. I feel it everywhere, my pussy, my ass, the pulse of my clit against my fingers.

It's pure ecstasy.

"Fuck. Shit. *Fuck*," Smith mutters, feeling it rack my body as I tighten around him.

He pulls out of me, ripping off the condom, and gives himself a few strokes until he's spilling his orgasm across my back.

Marking me.

Claiming me.

His. His. His.

I collapse into the bed, every single inch of my body numb. Smith falls into a heap beside me, trying to catch his breath. I have no idea how long we lie there, how long there's no other sound in the apartment except our heavy breaths.

Eventually, Smith pulls himself off the bed and pads into the bathroom. I hear him move around, washing his hands, then gurgling mouthwash. He returns quickly with a wet washcloth, gently wipes away the leftover lube on my ass, and proceeds to clean away the mess he made on my back.

He tosses the cloth back into the bathroom, then scoops me into his arms and wraps us both back under the blanket. He hauls me against his chest, hugging me close, and I snuggle into him. We stay like that for what feels like hours, the threat of sleep always looming just out of reach.

The sun clears the horizon, and the noises of the city begin. Only then do we make an effort to join the rest of the waking world.

Smith peers down at me, and I look up at him.

He grins. "Good morning."

I chuckle. "Good morning. Breakfast?"

He nods. "Let's order in."

It's a good thing he doesn't have practice today, because we spend the rest of the morning just like that.

Tori wasn't too happy when I called and told her I'd be working from home, but I didn't care. There was no way I would have been able to face her after last night and this morning. All she would have to do is raise one of those perfectly plucked eyebrows of hers, and I'd cave.

Of course, as soon as I got off the phone with her, Blake texted me wondering where the hell I was.

I hated lying to him, but I know I'd have hated having to face him even more.

We finally make our way from the bed to the couch at about two PM. We turn a movie on, but it's long forgotten when Smith makes me sit on the coffee table and finger myself to completion while he watches, refusing to touch me no matter how much I beg. After I come, he fucks me again.

We sit out on his patio at around four, and he lays me out on the lounger, then buries his face between my legs. He doesn't make love to me until I come twice.

"Are you hungry?" Smith asks at around seven, his fingers kneading my feet.

My stomach growls in response, and I realize then we haven't eaten since breakfast.

"Starving apparently," I say. "Should we order in again?"

"I was thinking of making some pasta. I have some chicken and veggies in the fridge. We can make something with that."

My brows lift. "You know how to like *cook* cook? Not just breakfast foods?"

He glares. "Well, breakfast is my specialty, but I'm an

almost forty-year-old bachelor, Emilia. I can't live off takeout forever. Of course I can cook. Can you?"

I lift my shoulder. "Some things. Not many, and not very well, to be honest."

He shoves my feet off his lap, then rises from the couch, holding his hand out for me. "Come on, then. Today we're going to learn."

I tip my head at him. "Can I use this in the profile?"

It's the first time either of us has mentioned work since our discussion this morning. It feels wrong to ask but also too good a piece of information to pass up.

He nods, and I slide my hand into his, letting him pull me to the kitchen.

He sets me on the counter next to him, talking me through how he preps and cuts the chicken. He throws a few different herbs and spices into the pan with plenty of olive oil, then gets started on making the sauce.

Watching him move through the kitchen in nothing but a pair of black sweats...it's hypnotizing. He throws together a completely home-cooked meal while carrying on a conversation with me and does it effortlessly all while looking like a GQ model.

It's ridiculous and unfair.

But damn am I thankful for the show.

When dinner is ready, Smith pulls me onto his lap and proceeds to feed me my entire meal. It feels so... intimate. I've never had someone take care of me the way he does, never had someone pay so much attention to me.

It's almost unnerving but also incredibly hot.

"I can't," I tell him as he tries to get me to eat another bite. "I'm stuffed."

He lifts a brow. "Not yet, but you can be."

I gape at him, a choked laugh sputtering out of me. "Owen Smith…that's naughty!"

He pins me with a stare. "Oh, *that's* what's naughty? Not you sucking cum off my cock while I fingered your ass not even two hours ago?"

I blush at his words.

"Don't get shy on me now," he says, pinching my sides playfully. "I have plans for you later."

I've never been so sexually satisfied yet still so hungry for more in my life. Any time I think there's no way I could possibly orgasm again, Smith proves me wrong.

"How is your refractory period even this good?"

He narrows his eyes at my obvious reference to his age. "Making up for lost time."

"Making up for…" I roll my eyes. "Please. Like *you've* lost any time. You're a damn NHL star—you can get laid whenever."

A dark look crosses his face, and he grabs my chin, pulling my face to his.

"First, don't roll your eyes at me. Second"—his grip tightens, not enough to hurt but just enough to be a warning—"I'm making up for lost time."

I…I don't understand what he's saying. Smith is attractive, always making lists of hockey's hottest eligible bachelors. He has women throwing themselves at him all the time. Hell, it happened in the coffee shop just before Christmas, so I don't understand what lost time he's—

I gasp.

"You...haven't been with anyone since me?"

He shakes his head, releasing my face, his hand falling back to my hip. "No."

"That's...over two years."

"Trust me, I'm aware."

"But why?" I blurt out. "Why wait that long? That's..."

He lifts his shoulders. "Nothing ever felt right. What about...you?" He swallows, almost like he hates asking the question. "I'm not going to be upset if you have. I—"

"No," I cut him off.

His eyes spark. "No?"

I shake my head. "No. I tried. I went on *a lot* of dates." His grip on my hip tightens at that, but I keep going. "There was nothing though. Nothing felt as good as..."

You.

I leave it unsaid, but I know he's aware of what I mean.

This. Us.

He blows out a relieved breath. "I understand."

The reality of that settles over us, because we both know no matter how good it feels, it can't last, not while we're in the positions we're in.

"I...I should go," I say, trying to push from his lap.

He doesn't let me move.

191

"Smith…"

"Do you want to go?"

I sigh, dropping my forehead to his. "I should. We both know that."

"There are a lot of things we apparently *should* do, Emilia, but it doesn't mean we have to do them." He squeezes my hip. "Just fun, remember?"

"Just fun."

"Good. So, let me ask again, do you want to go?"

"No."

"Then stay."

And I do.

CHAPTER 17

SMITH

She stayed.

I'm supposed to be thinking about hockey. The puck, the net, where I need to be on the ice to cover my man— that is *all* I should be thinking about, especially with a game this evening, but I can't get the image of Emilia on her knees in the shower this morning out of my head because she stayed.

She's been over at my house every night this week and has stayed over all but one of them, including this morning when I woke up with my cock against her ass and her pressing back, seeking my touch.

I obliged, of course, and then we took a shower, where she sucked me off and made me late for the morning skate.

We've kept to our agreement of living inside a bubble. When we're at my apartment, we're just us. She's not the girl waiting for the promotion, and I'm not the guy who plays hockey for her uncle. We're just Emilia and Owen and we're just having fun; that's it. It's uncomplicated and easy, and for the first time in a long time, I'm feeling good.

"You're chipper." Miller flops down onto the bench beside me. "Get your dick wet?"

"Miller!" Lowell chides as he walks by, shaking his head at the kid for his crudeness.

"Pretty sure I heard him whistling when he walked in this morning," Rhodes comments, dropping down across from us.

I glare at him. "I was not." I turn to Miller. "And I'm not chipper."

"Well, you're not *my* kind of chipper," he says, "but you're chipper by your standards."

"I am not."

His face scrunches up. "Not right now you're definitely not with all of your arguing and glowering." He shakes his head. "I take it back. You're clearly not getting laid, but you should. You need it."

"You offering?" I tease.

"Like you could handle me," he mutters before storming off, and I feel good knowing I somehow managed to annoy the most obnoxious guy on the team. I'm glad that maybe—just maybe—I've thrown him off.

"He's right, you know," our goalie says, fidgeting with his equipment. "You're different lately."

I don't spend a lot of time with Greer outside the rink. A few shindigs here and there, but I wouldn't say we're close by any stretch of the imagination. I highly doubt he's a good judge of how much I have or haven't changed.

"How would you know?"

He shrugs. "I'm observant."

That's one word for what he is. "Uh-huh."

He peeks up at me, then back at his pads. "It started around whenever that ginger in media began coming around more often. Whatever"—another glance, this one a lot more suggestive than the other—"*thing* it is you're working on with her, it's definitely changed something in you."

I barely fight the urge to roll my eyes. "Right. And this change would be…"

"He was right," Rhodes speaks up, pointing toward the door Miller disappeared through. "You're chipper."

I grit my teeth together. "I'm really not."

Rhodes tips his head to the side, watching me. "Hmm."

"What?"

"Nothing."

"That didn't sound like nothing."

"Well, it was." He shrugs. "I'm hitting the ice."

I glare after him.

"Smith!"

I snap my head up to find Coach Martin standing in the doorway, hands on his hips, a serious look on his face.

Oh fuck. He knows.

I'm dead. Or worse, off the team. They're benching me for breaking the rules.

"Uh, what's up, Coach?" I try for nonchalant and hope to fuck I don't sound like I'm about to have a very real panic attack.

"I think you know what's up—you're avoiding me, and I know why."

My heart pounds so hard in my chest that there's no way Coach Martin doesn't hear it. The very real fear of having a heart attack—which would just do wonders for my old man status—hits me.

"Board drills!" He laughs. "I know they're your favorite." He claps his hands together. "Come on. Chop, chop. Meet me on the ice in five."

He walks away, and I sink back into my cubby, blowing out a relieved breath.

He doesn't know. *Thank fuck* he doesn't know.

Greer laughs. I almost forgot he was there.

He shakes his head.

"What?" I bark out, annoyed with him.

"Nothing. Just…a theory."

"A theory?"

"Yeah," he says, rising to his skates. "About you and that hot little redhead."

I push off the bench, and yeah, Greer is a big dude, but I'm bigger. I tower over him, looking down my nose at him and that stupid fucking smirk on his face.

"What about her?" Even I hear the jealousy in those three words.

I don't like him noticing her. I don't like him talking

about her. I don't even like him being in the same room as her.

My reaction makes him laugh harder, and my brows slam together even tighter.

"It's just interesting that your mood changed when you started working with her…almost as if she has something to do with it."

He lifts a brow, waiting for me to tell him he's wrong.

I don't.

"Hmm. Interesting." He steps away and around me, checking his shoulder against mine. When he's at the door, he pauses and looks back. "You know, Miller was wrong. You don't need to get laid—you already are." He walks away, leaving me standing there fuming.

I want to run after him and deny everything, tell him he's wrong and there's nothing going on between Emilia and me.

But it'd be a fucking lie and we both know it.

"Please tell me he's joking." I whirl around to see Lowell standing at the door. He's resting on his stick, his watchful gaze burning into me. "Are you screwing around with Emilia?"

"It's not what Greer thinks." The lie tumbles out easily, and I pray Lowell believes it.

"Are you sure about that? Because you look pretty damn guilty to me right now." He shakes his head. "You know what? I don't care whether it's true or not. I don't want to hear about it. Just whatever it is…fix it."

He stalks away, still shaking his head at me.

He's right. What Emilia and I are doing…it's a stupid game, a dangerous one. I know better than to play it.

I'm not on any leader boards for penalty minutes, but I always did have a knack for finding myself in the sin bin, and if this all blows up in our faces, that's exactly where I'm headed.

I just hope it's worth it.

I've done a lot of hard things in my lifetime, battled at the boards for long torturous hours, played games where I walked out with broken bones, and have just generally put myself through hell, all in the name of a sport.

But this? It has to be one of the most difficult things I've done.

"This is pure torture," Greer says from beside me, and for once, I agree with the guy. "I fucking hate kids. Can't stand the little crotch goblins."

Well, that part I don't agree with. I don't have any feelings toward children one way or the other. They're cute sometimes, but other times, they're annoying little shits. As far as having any, I think I could take it or leave it.

But having to attend a baby shower where there are women *oohing* and *aahing* over *all* things baby—it's kind of a bit much.

For the most part, Hollis and Lowell have kept this whole thing low-key, but there is still a horde of women who won't stop squealing over all the *tiny wittle baby cwothes*. It's grating on my last damn nerve.

"Is it too soon to leave?" he says.

"Unfortunately. I need a drink," I mutter, heading for the little bar they graciously provided for us folk who can drink. I pour myself a glass of whiskey, then turn to find Lowell and Miller standing near the doorway to the room. Lowell looks like he's about two seconds away from driving his fist into Miller's face. Whatever Miller did or said, I'm sure it would be deserved.

"Go. Away," Lowell says to the kid as I approach.

"Roger that."

Miller takes off faster than he's ever moved before.

I follow Lowell's gaze to Hollis, who is surrounded by Ryan, Emilia, and Harper, and several other players' wives. He looks like he's about to stalk across the room, throw his pregnant woman over his shoulder, and carry her away from all the prying eyes.

I get it. I've been wanting to do the same with Emilia since we got here.

Even though she woke up in my bed this morning, we arrived separately so we wouldn't draw any suspicion. We've also spent the afternoon ignoring one another, which has been harder than I thought it would be. A few times I almost reached out and brushed some hair off her shoulder, but then I realized at the last moment that I couldn't do that, especially not with all the watchful eyes around.

Pretending at the rink is one thing because we're at

work, but here? Surrounded by our friends who are so open with one another? It's hard to remember she's not mine and, no matter how badly I want her there, she doesn't belong at my side.

"Those are some rather territorial vibes you're giving off about somebody you're not even dating," I say, taking Miller's place. "Because you're allegedly still not dating, right?"

He ignores me, and I laugh.

"Come on, man. You can't really tell me you're not dating—not when you're looking at her like that."

He's staring out at Hollis like she's an angel walking the earth. It's funny to see how much he's changed over the last five months since finding out about the baby, from anti-commitment and never letting anyone come over to his place to looking awfully cozy with the woman carrying his child and hosting a damn baby shower at his house.

He glares over at me. "I don't know what you're talking about. There's nothing going on."

"Uh-huh. Sure. Right. Nothing at all."

"What's going on with you and Emilia? Is that nothing too?" he shoots right back at me.

I snap my mouth closed, feeling a lot less like teasing him.

"That's what I thought," he mutters.

"Nothing is going on with me and…" I hesitate, afraid to say her name, because if I do, I know it's going to come out sounding entirely too sweet. Lowell's not stupid. He'll pick up on it. *"Her,"* I finish.

He scoffs. "You can't even say her name."

"I can too."

"Prove it."

I tip my chin up. "No. I don't need to prove shit to you."

"Weird. I don't need to prove shit to you either."

He shoves past me, disappearing into the kitchen.

I want to be annoyed with him, but I guess fair is fair. I'm not exactly being forthcoming about what's going on with Emilia, so I can't expect him to open up to me with what's happening with him and Hollis.

I can say though that he's holding back for no reason at all. It's clear he's falling for her and she's falling for him, and not just because she's having his child. There's a love there that's lurking deeper beneath the surface. I saw it at Harper and Collin's wedding last summer when they met.

I wish he would realize what's right in front of him and take advantage of it, embrace it. I sure as hell wish I could.

Emilia throws her head back, laughing at something Miller says. The sunlight pouring into the room catches her red hair just right, almost making it look gold. The strands are swept up in her usual bun and my fingers itch to pull it down and wrap it around my fist. She's gorgeous, and I wish so fucking badly I could march across this room and kiss her.

Claim her.

Let everyone know she's *mine*.

I take a step and—

"Heya, kid," our head coach, Heller, says, stopping me in my tracks.

I relax, lifting my chin at the older man. "Coach."

He's on the smaller side, but it doesn't mean shit. Back in his days of playing in the NHL, he was known for being an enforcer, tough as nails and ready to throw down with the best of them. Sometimes I think his smaller stature came in handy during the fights. He was little enough to move quickly and be able to duck, but also sturdy enough to keep his skates upright.

"Sometimes I miss this part of it," he says, looking out at the group gathered. "Being part of a team, you know? These found families. It's tough when it's all gone."

Family.

That is what we have here. Even though Greer pisses me off and Miller's obnoxious on a good day, we're still a family, and we have each other's back. We're there for each other through all the trials and tribulations.

Once my contract expires, does this expire too? I hate the idea of losing this as much as I hate the idea of losing.

Coach clears his throat. "Ah, ignore the ramblings of an old man. I'm taking off, getting out of your hair because I know it's no fun with Coach hanging around."

He tips his head toward the rest of the crowd. "Keep an eye on these kids, will ya?"

"Shouldn't you be telling your captain that?"

"Would, but I can't seem to find him *or* his gal." He does his best to fight a knowing grin. Lowell might think he's fooling everyone saying he doesn't have feelings for Hollis, but if even Coach is picking up on it, it's a losing battle. "Figured I'd task that job to you with you being the oldest. Besides, you're a lot less trouble than any of these young people. You're the one I never have to worry about."

Bile works its way up the back of my throat and I swallow it down, trying not to vomit all over Coach's nice dress shirt. *If he only knew...*

"I'll keep an eye on them," I say quietly.

He claps me on the shoulder. "Knew I could count on you. Tell Lowell and Hollis thank you for the invite."

"Will do."

He gives me another smile before disappearing through the house.

I watch as he goes, trying to swallow back the guilt that's eating at me. Coach has done so much for me, and how am I repaying him? By lying to him? Breaking rules put in place for a good reason? I should be ashamed of myself.

But I'm not.

I'm not, because Emilia? She feels right.

"Hey." That combination of lavender and vanilla I can't seem to get enough of hits me. "Everything okay?"

Her eyes flick to where Coach Heller is going, and I know what she's really asking: *Does he know?*

With a quick glance around the room to make sure nobody is watching—and no one is—I grab Emilia's hand and haul her down the hallway into an empty bathroom. She lets out a little squeak as I pull her in and press her against the door, framing her body with my own, a knee pressed between her legs.

"Owen, I—"

I don't let her finish that sentence. Instead, I cover her mouth with my own, kissing away every last worry she could possibly be having right now. I shouldn't be doing this. Not here, not now.

But I can't help it. I have to touch her. It's torture sitting on the other side of the room watching her laugh and smile with everyone else.

I want her laughs. I want her smiles.

I want *her*.

Need her.

Crave her.

I should be concerned that I'm losing control and doing this here, but I don't care, not when I have her under me. I don't stop kissing her, not even when she's mewling against me and rubbing her pussy along my thigh.

I'd bet at least a year's salary if I were to step away from her right now, there'd be a dark spot on my jeans from her soaking-wet cunt. I slide my hand up her thigh, pushing the dress she's wearing up around her waist, and run a single knuckle over her.

I wrench my mouth from hers, kissing my way down her chin, over her neck, then back to her lips again, all while running my finger over her pussy.

"Fuck, Emilia," I mutter. "You're so damn wet for me."

I shove her panties to the side and, without warning, slide two fingers inside of her.

"*Oh god*," she moans, and it's loud, so loud I clamp my hand against her mouth.

She stares up at me with wide, lustful eyes, then bears down on my fingers, and I curse myself for what I started as she begins to fuck herself on my hand.

She doesn't take her eyes off me, riding me, moaning again as I hook them inside of her, hitting that spot I know she loves. She picks up her pace, riding me harder and faster, and I wish it were my cock buried in her instead of my fingers.

"You're so beautiful, Emilia," I tell her, my eyes on hers. "So gorgeous. You're doing such a good job fucking my fingers, you know that?"

She nods.

"Fuck, you need to see this. You need to see how good you look."

Another nod.

I spin us until we're facing the mirror, and I hold her in front of me, letting her see what I'm seeing.

"Hold your dress up," I murmur in her ear. "Look."

She listens, lifting her dress until it's around her waist, her eyes dropping to where she rides my hand. Her bottom lip is trapped between her teeth, sweat beading at her temples, her hair a wild mess.

She's stunning, and she's getting close. I can feel it in the way she's squeezing me, desperate for release.

"Can you take more, sweetheart?"

She doesn't speak; she can't. She simply nods, and I slide a third finger into her pussy. She squeezes around me, a low, soft moan escaping her. When she tries to close her eyes and drop her head, I don't let her. I wrap my hand around her throat with my free hand, lifting her head back up until she's looking in the mirror.

"Watch the way you fuck yourself, Emilia. Look how beautiful you are."

Her eyes are on her pussy, and when I press my thumb to her clit, she's shaking in my arms, falling apart on my fingers. I pull her lips to mine, swallowing her moans with my kiss again, hoping nobody can hear us.

She rides me through her orgasm, slowing and steadying her movements until the final shocks are gone. I slowly slide my fingers from her pussy, and she whimpers as I lazily pet her, allowing her a moment to catch her breath.

"I wish I could taste you right now," I say in her ear. "When we get home, I'm going to bury my face between your thighs and lick your pussy until it's squeezing my tongue."

She shivers at the idea, looking every bit like she's

ready to go again. I'm about to say fuck it and drop to my knees when the door handle rattles.

Emilia lets out a loud squeak, turning into my arms.

"Oh! Shit! Sorry!" Rhodes calls from the other side of the door. "Didn't realize anyone was in here. My bad."

"It's cool, man," I call out.

"Oh…Smith? Thought that high-pitched scream was a chick for a moment."

"Fuck off."

Rhodes laughs. "Have you seen Emilia? I think Ryan was looking for her."

Emilia's eyes widen, and with her hair all over the place, she looks wild.

"No," I lie, motioning for her to fix it. "Last I saw her she was taking a phone call outside."

"Huh. Okay, I'll tell Ryan. You, uh, going to be much longer? I really have to take a leak."

"Can you not keep talking to me when I have my dick in my hand?"

"Like I haven't seen it before," Rhodes mutters. "I'll just use the other bathroom."

He retreats, and I wait several moments before turning to Emilia, who is still trying to tame her mane.

"That was entirely too close," she whispers, shoving stray hairs into place.

"I didn't hear you complaining."

Her cheeks pinken at my words. She turns, facing me.

"Well, no, of course not—but that's beside the point. We have bigger fish to fry."

"Yeah, like the fact that Rhodes now thinks I scream like a girl."

She narrows her eyes. "What's wrong with a girl scream?"

"My scream is very, *very* deep, thank you very much."

She rolls her lips together, patting my chest. "I'm sure it is. We should head back before someone realizes I'm not in fact outside on the phone." She gives me a look for that lie.

"What was I supposed to do? Tell him you're in here about to get your pussy eaten?"

She makes a noise that's halfway between a groan and a moan. "Smith!"

I grin. "Look, I'll go out first, then you wait a few minutes and follow. Sound good?"

She nods, shoving me toward the door.

I grab the handle, but before I open the door, I look back at her. "Oh, and, Emilia?"

"Hmm?"

"I intend to make good on that promise."

Her face flames red as I close the door, and I swear I hear her mutter, "What the hell have I gotten myself into?"

I've been asking myself the same thing.

CHAPTER 18

Smith: Please tell me your night was better than mine.

Emilia: I'm sorry about the loss. That one was brutal.

Smith: Getting shut out is never good, but when it's a team that's 30th in the league? Hurts.

Emilia: If it makes you feel any better, I've been at the office since eight AM.

Smith: Are you still there?

Emilia: Yes.

· · ·

Smith: What the hell for?

Emilia: Tori. She needs me to write up a proposal for a campaign with a local charity, and she needs it by tomorrow. She sprung it on me right before puck drop, so I had to juggle the game and now this.

Smith: Screw that. Leave.

Emilia: I will soon. I just have a few more things to put together and then I'm good.

Smith: Emilia…

Emilia: That's my name. Don't wear it out.

Emilia: Unless it's in bed. *wink*

Smith: I'm being serious.

Emilia: So am I. *double wink*

. . .

Smith: Wouldn't that just be a blink?

Emilia: No! I winked twice!

Smith: You really should go home. Finish it in the morning.

Emilia: I already have stuff to do tomorrow morning.

Smith: I'm sorry. I wish I was there to help.

Emilia: I don't. Your version of "helping" is to get me naked.

Emilia: Actually, I lied. I do wish you were here.

Smith: That's what I thought.

Smith: At least text me when you get home.

. . .

Emilia: You're kind of bossy, you know.

Smith: You like it.

Emilia: I do. Possibly a bit too much.

Smith: No such thing as too much.

Smith: Now, go work. Get your shit done and get home. Within the next hour, please.

Emilia: Yes, sir.

Smith: You're playing with fire, Emilia.

Emilia: What are you going to do? Glare menacingly at your flip phone?

Smith: Flip phone??

. . .

Smith: I'm not that old!

Emilia: Whatever you say, gramps.

Smith: I swear, I'm spanking your ass when I get back.

Emilia: Promises, promises.

Emilia: *kissy-face emoji*

Emilia: Don't hate me, but when you get home, we need more content.

Smith: MORE?

Smith: How many damn videos do we need for this thing?

. . .

Emilia: A lot.

Emilia: We post daily, and not everything is for the player profile. Some of it is just for the team.

Smith: No.

Emilia: Please??

Smith: Fine.

Smith: But for a price.

Emilia: *sigh*

Emilia: You want to see my boobs, don't you?

Smith: Yes.

Emilia: Fine.

. . .

Emilia: You're such a guy, you know that?

Smith: Yep. Well aware.

Smith: What are the videos about?

Emilia: It's a Q&A series. We have fans submit questions, then we filter through them. It will only be about ten.

Emilia: For the profile, I mean.

Emilia: It'll be at least five videos for the team.

Smith: FIVE?!?

Emilia:

Smith: I want more than boobs.

. . .

Emilia: Fine. I'll send both tits, then.

Smith: You were only going to send one???

Smith: That's just mean.

Smith: Tease.

Emilia: Damn right I am!

Emilia: What am I getting out of sending you a tit pic?

Smith: THE VIDEOS!

Emilia: Those are for the team, not me.

Smith: You make a valid point, but I really feel like that's cheating.

. . .

Emilia: Oh, it definitely is.

Emilia: But you're going to let me cheat anyway.

Smith: I am?

Emilia: Yes. Because I'm cute.

Smith: Hmm.

Smith: Fair.

Smith: You're kind of sassy today, you know that?

Emilia: I know.

Smith: Well, as long as you're aware.

Emilia: On a scale of 1-10, how good of a dancer are you?

Smith: 0

Emilia: That's not a valid answer.

Smith: -1

Emilia: Smith...

Smith: I am not dancing.

Smith: Never.

Smith: Ever.

Smith: Keep fucking dreaming.

Emilia: Not even for the team?

. . .

Smith: Not a chance.

Emilia: BOO!

Smith: Boo me all you want. It's not happening.

Emilia: It will make really good content though…

Smith: I don't care. Dancing is where I draw the line.

Emilia: Lowell's dancing.

Smith: What dirt do you have on him?

Emilia: Enough.

Smith: I'm curious but I know you well enough to know that if I want details, I'll have to make an exchange and I'm still not dancing.

. . .

Emilia: Ugh. Fine.

Emilia: *crosses off next ten ideas*

Smith: I'm sure you'll come up with something else.

Emilia: And here I was, ready to offer up blow jobs in exchange for content.

Smith: ...

Smith: What kind of dancing?

Smith: Be honest...

Smith: Does it make me an old man if I order oatmeal for breakfast?

. . .

Emilia: Yes.

Smith: You're supposed to say no.

Emilia: Well, I don't want to lie to you so...

Emilia: Yes.

Emilia: It's a total old person food.

Smith: Watch your tone, little girl.

Emilia: It's text. You can't hear my tone.

Smith: Trust me, I can.

Emilia: Can you hear this?

Smith: You just rolled your eyes, didn't you?

· · ·

Emilia: Possibly. *grins*

Smith: I thought you youngins were supposed to show your elders respect.

Emilia: I don't think you "respected" me very much the last time I saw you.

Smith: I did and that's exactly why I did what I did.

Emilia: Okay. That's fair.

Emilia: Why are you worried about being "old" for ordering oatmeal?

Emilia: Wait. Let me guess. Miller?

Smith: No. That shithead Greer.

Emilia: You don't like your goalie?

. . .

Smith: Of course I like my goalie. But only on the ice.

Smith: He's a cocky little prick.

Emilia: But also totally saving your asses this year.

Smith: Whose side are you on here?

Emilia: Yours. Totally yours.

Emilia: But...am I lying?

Smith: No.

Emilia: That totally killed you to say, didn't it?

Smith: Yes.

Emilia: You'll be fine.

· · ·

Emilia: I'll make sure I kiss you back to life when you get home tomorrow.

Smith: Start with my dick, please.

Emilia: We'll see.

Emilia: *whispers* That's a lie. I totally will.

CHAPTER 19

EMILIA

"You're telling me you've lived here nearly three years and you have never been here before?"

"Nope. Not once."

He presses his hand to his chest. "That is a travesty."

"Does it count that I've at least had the donuts before? Sometimes there's a box floating around the break room."

"It makes it better, but trust me, they're even better fresh." He pats his flat stomach. "My mouth is watering just thinking about them."

"Calm down. I'm sure there's not that *big* of a difference."

He pins me with a stare that tells me I'm wrong.

It's a random Wednesday in February, so I'm really not expecting the line standing before me. It's at least six customers deep when we step up to the back.

"Is it always like this?"

Smith nods. "Pretty much."

"Wow. I didn't realize it was this popular."

"Even when you want to, Scout's hard to resist."

"Scout?"

He points to the woman behind the register of the adorable baby-blue food truck. "That's Scout. She's the owner, baker, and best donut maker." He grins at his rhyme. "But seriously, she's great."

"You're on a first-name basis with her?"

He shrugs. "I eat a lot of donuts."

Scout notices Smith pointing her way and waves. Just about everyone in line ahead of us turns to see who she's waving at, and many of them begin talking behind their hands when they realize it's a Comets player. Smith pulls his hat down low, but it's pointless. Everyone already knows it's him.

I take note of the fact that so many people here know who he is and put a little extra space between us just in case. If Smith notices, he doesn't say anything.

One by one, people in line start coming up to Smith and asking for an autograph. He's more than happy to do it, and I really appreciate that about him. By the time we make it to the front to order, Scout's giving Smith a sheepish grin.

"Sorry. Didn't mean to draw attention."

Smith shrugs. "They would have noticed me eventually. Always happens."

"It really does. You hockey players are good for business." She turns to me, beaming. "Hi. I don't think we've met before. I'm Scout."

"Emilia. Your donuts are delicious, but I've

226

unfortunately never had the chance to make it here before."

"Well, welcome to Scout's Sweets." She waves her hand around. "It's not much, but it's mine."

"Not much? This place is so cute! I love the little sandbox and the mobile library."

Her eyes light up. "I'm a huge book lover."

"Boys in books are just better," I say.

"Yes! That's exactly what I always say!"

"I take great offense to that," Smith interjects.

Scout and I both roll our eyes at him because he just doesn't get it.

"Anyway," Scout says, "what can I get for you today?" She points to Smith. "I'm assuming your usual Granny Apple donuts and coffee?"

I try not to laugh at the irony of his donut order.

"Please, and then whatever Emilia here wants," he tells her, pulling his wallet from his back pocket.

I tap my fingers against my chin, perusing the menu. "I've had your glazed donuts several times before, but I'm feeling a bit adventurous today. Any suggestions?"

"Do you prefer chocolate or vanilla?"

"Chocolate. Always."

"While I love all the donuts I make, I have a soft spot for my Pretty Please donut. It's a chocolate base with cherry frosting."

"Perfect. I'll take two of those and an iced coffee with—"

"Cream and three sugars," Smith finishes for me, handing his card over to Scout.

Her eyes bounce between the two of us, and I'm not loving how perceptive they are, or the knowing grin she gives us as she charges the card.

"Go have a seat," she tells us. "I'll bring your order out for you."

Smith's hand goes to my lower back, and I wonder if he even notices—I sure do—as he steers us toward one of the few unoccupied picnic tables toward the back of the lot.

I try not to laugh at how ridiculous Smith looks sliding into it. He's so big he makes it look like he's sitting on kids' furniture instead of at a regular-sized table.

"Don't laugh at me just because I ate my vegetables and you didn't. Not my fault you stopped growing."

"Hey, I'll have you know I am *above* average height for women, thank you very much. I ate my vegetables too. You're just freakishly gigantic."

"In many areas."

"Smith!" I admonish, looking around to make sure nobody heard him, but it's pointless. We're practically all alone back here. I have a feeling he chose this spot for that exact reason. "This is supposed to be a work breakfast, you know."

"Does the working start now, or did it start earlier when I was eating your—"

I slap my hand over his mouth.

"Not another word," I say, sharpening my gaze.

I don't have to see his mouth to know he's grinning at me. I can see it in his eyes.

I peel my hand away just as Scout makes her way over to us, two coffees and a box of donuts in her hand.

"Here you go," she says, setting our order down on the table. She turns to Smith and holds what looks like a piece of construction paper out to him. "And this is for you from Macie."

A small smile plays on Smith's lips as he takes the paper. "Thanks."

"Don't thank her yet. Just wait until you see the picture she drew of you." Scout laughs. "Enjoy the donuts." She practically skips back to the food truck, and I nod toward the paper.

"What's that she gave you?"

Smith grins, looking down at what appears to be a homemade card. "Last year, Scout's eight-year-old niece, Macie, needed a sponsor for her soccer team so they could afford to get their uniforms made, so I covered it for them. This season, I just outright sponsored the whole year." He shrugs. "It was no big deal."

He says it so casually, like to him it really wasn't a big deal, and I'm sure that is the case. But for the little girl and her soccer team, I know it meant the world having a famous athlete cover things for them so they don't have to worry about expenses and can just play.

"Anyway, since then, she's been dropping thank-you cards with Scout every few weeks, so I began sending her notes back and drawing pictures in them. It's silly stuff mostly, her as a superhero, that kind of thing. At first, it was fun, then she started taking some…creative liberties." He frowns. "Like at Christmas. That one was sweet…until you opened it."

"What'd it say?"

"It wasn't so much what it said but how she drew me. There were lines all over my face, and when I asked what they were, she looked me straight in the eyes and said *wrinkles*."

I laugh, not just at the card and what the bold little girl wrote, but also at the way Smith's brows slam together. I'm almost certain the wrinkles forming from his scowling are exactly what she drew.

"Let's hope this one is better," he mumbles, flipping open the bright orange paper. He gasps. "That little shit!"

"What is it?" I strain my neck, trying to see what's on the card.

"Scout!" he yells, and she pops her head up. He waves the card. "Tell that little turd niece of yours that payback is a bitch!"

Scout just laughs, shaking her head.

"What is it?" I ask again, and Smith shoves the card at me, glaring at it like it's offensive.

He's right. The front is innocent enough. It just says THANK YOU in sprawling, crooked letters. But when I flip it open, I immediately know what it is that has him so upset.

Laughter bubbles out of me, which just causes Smith's scowl to deepen even more.

"It's not funny," he grumbles.

"Oh, but it is."

"Is not." He snatches the card back, tucking it into the inside pocket of his jacket. "She's eight. She's not supposed to be that mean." He shakes his head, and it takes everything I have not to point out the way the sun catches the gray in his hair that's sticking out of his cap. "A fucking cane. Little shit drew me with a *cane* like I'm some old man or something."

I do a poor job of trying to conceal another laugh, earning me yet another scowl.

"Come on, it's cute!"

"It's mean. Like I don't already get enough shit from the guys on the team."

"Yeah, but they do it because they love you. They don't really care that you're old."

"And do you?" he asks. "Care that I'm older than you?"

Our age gap isn't something we've really discussed. We're both aware there's a ten-year difference between us, but we don't talk about it. Just like we don't talk about what any of this truly means.

I try not to think about that though.

"No. Not at all. Do *you* care that I'm younger than you?"

"No. I mean, that first night…" He shakes his head from side to side. "Yeah, maybe then, but only because I knew I shouldn't have been taking *anyone* home, let alone someone ten years younger than me. But…nah. I haven't really given it much thought since."

I haven't thought about it much either. I'm sure someone out there would have an issue with it. But we're both adults, and we're both thoroughly enjoying whatever this is that we're doing. That should be all that matters.

"Good. Then it's settled: you don't care that I'm a young spring chicken, and I don't care that you groan every time you stand."

He gives me yet another glare as he peels open our box of donuts. He holds one of mine out to me. "Eat."

I don't think twice about leaning forward and taking a bite. The warmth is the first thing I notice, then the delicious cherry frosting mixed with the chocolate. I can't help the moan that leaves my lips.

Smith doesn't miss it, his eyes darkening for a whole different reason now.

"See?" he says. "I told you fresh was better."

"You were right," I say, taking the donut from his fingers and taking another bite. The rich flavor explodes over my tongue. "So good."

"Scout's got talent, that's for sure. But that niece of hers…" He shakes his head, digging into his own breakfast.

He gets one donut down before someone approaches the table and asks for an autograph. He grins, agreeing easily, never once making it seem like they're interrupting his breakfast. I'm so used to being around the game all the time that I forget the guys on the Comets are idols to some people.

I mean, I'm sure their opinions of them would change if they had to smell just how quickly those grown men can stink up a locker room and witness some of the less-than-stellar habits some of them have, but still. They're famous hockey players, and people all over the world are watching them.

At one point he even takes the hat off his own head and signs it for a young kid, then jogs back out to his truck for a new one. I love seeing him in this environment, interacting outside of the rink when he's not obligated to do it. He's so patient and kind with every person who approaches, especially the children, and it's making my heart do funny things to see him like this.

The more time we spend together, the more I'm really starting to like so many things about him. He might think all he has going for him is his hockey skills, but he's so much more than that.

Somehow, I manage to remember to snap a few photos of Smith signing things for the team's Instagram account, and I also take some pictures on the fans' phones.

"You're really good at this," I comment when the crowd at the truck thins out. "Doing the whole famous hockey player thing. The kids really look up to you, especially the young ones who play. Have you thought about doing something with them after you're done in the NHL?"

He tips his head. "Like what?"

I shrug. "I don't know, like coaching or something? I've seen you on the ice with the guys. Yeah, Lowell might be the captain, but the guys listen to you just as much as they do him."

"Only because I'm the oldest."

I shake my head. "No, that's not the only reason. You just have this…presence about you. Like you demand attention, but not in a scary way. It's natural—sort of like the pull my uncle has. I think it could make you a really good coach."

"Coaching?" he mutters, pondering it. "I haven't really considered that."

"Have you given any thought to what you want to do when you're out?"

His lips tug down into a frown, his eyes sliding out to the little lake that butts up to the parking lot. "I've tried not to think about it too much, you know? Just trying to live in the moment, enjoy it while it lasts."

Like a lot of aging athletes, there's been speculation for a few seasons now about whether or not Smith was going to retire, especially after the Comets won the Cup. He got the big trophy, so he'd be done for sure then, right? But no, he stuck around. With his contract expiring at the end of this year, the talk has really picked up again.

I can understand why he doesn't want to look that far

ahead though. I'm sure it's scary. Hockey is all he's ever known in his adult life. Moving beyond that is going to be hard.

"Is that...Miller?"

I look to where Smith's staring off across the parking lot and squint, trying to get a better look at the guy who has a hat pulled down low and a pair of aviators covering his eyes. If I didn't see him so often, I probably wouldn't look twice, which is likely why nobody is staring him down like they did Smith.

"Shit," Smith mutters. "That is him."

"Should we try to sneak away?" I ask.

"Nah. Kid is oblivious—probably won't even notice us. Besides, we can always just say we're working on the player profile if he spots us."

"We *are* working on it. That's why we're here and why Tori gave me the morning away from the office."

Smith lifts a brow. "Are you going to include the 'work' we did this morning in the player profile?"

I try not to blush thinking of how he tugged me into his apartment and did some *very* unprofessional things to me before he drove us here to one of his favorite spots in the city.

"I think I'll leave that out," I mutter, and he laughs.

Miller, not looking our way at all, struts up to the register, a smile plastered on his face. Even from here, I can spot Scout's blush, and I can't say I blame her. Miller's charming and—not that I'd say this out loud to

Smith—hot. It's no wonder Scout is looking at him like she is.

He places his order with a grin, probably being typical Miller and flirting his ass off with her. Scout turns away for a moment and gets his order ready. She's grinning at him again as she hands him a box of donuts and two coffees. I don't miss the way she stares longingly after him as he makes his way across the parking lot.

He doesn't head for his car, though. He walks right by it and crosses the street.

At the intersection, a man is sitting there with a sign that reads *ANYTHING HELPS*. Miller sits down on the ground next to him, hands him a coffee, and opens the box of donuts. The man takes one, and Miller takes another. They sit there talking animatedly for several minutes like they're old friends swapping stories or something.

Smith and I watch the whole thing, not saying a word.

After Miller gets up, waves goodbye to the man, and leaves, Smith turns to me and says, "*That's* who your player profile should have been about. Not me."

"The fans voted."

"Bullshit. Miller was the one who wrote my name in."

I wince. "Yeah, about that...I kind of know."

"Wait, you do?"

"Yeah, Miller came to my office one day and confessed everything, said he felt bad and didn't think you wanted to be part of it because you were stomping around extra grumpy, and he didn't want it messing with your game."

Smith snorts. "Oh, I was pissed all right. Probably more for reasons he didn't understand." He waves a hand between us. "But still pissed."

That same silence that always falls between us at any reminder of how temporary this is comes again.

It's interrupted when Scout stops at the end of the table.

"I'm heading out for an appointment, and my sister is going to take over for a few." She hitches her thumb toward the truck. "Just wanted to make sure you guys don't need anything else before I go."

Smith defers to me for the answer.

"Oh, no," I say, waving my hand. "I think we're good. Excellent recommendation to get the Pretty Please. That cherry icing was *amazing*."

"Thank you. I think it's one of my best ones." She beams proudly. "Anyway, I need to run. It was great to meet you, Emilia. I always love it when the guys start bringing their girlfriends here. It means things are getting serious."

"We're not dating," I say quickly, probably a little *too* quickly if the way Smith's head snaps up is any indication. "This is just for work."

Her mouth opens as she looks back and forth between Smith and me, and I can feel him staring a hole into the side of my head. I refuse to meet his stare, knowing full well if I look at him, I'll be giving entirely too much away.

"Oh. I just thought…" She rolls her lips together, shaking her head. "Never mind what I thought. My bad."

"No worries. Speaking of…do you mind if we film a few videos here? The Comets media department is highlighting Smith, and I'd love to include one of his favorite spots in some of the posts. We'll tag you in everything too."

"Oh, of course!" She claps her hands together, then grins brightly at Smith. "That's amazing for you!" The smile he gives her back doesn't reach his eyes, but if Scout notices, she doesn't comment. "Feel free to shoot wherever. You have my full permission for everything. And if you need anything—refill, more donuts, whatever —just let Stevie know and she'll get it. On the house, of course."

"Thanks," I tell her. "That's really nice of you."

"Oh, please. It's nothing. I'm sure Lowell has a lot to do with it since we went to high school together, but the Comets are always here supporting me and bringing in so many customers, so it's the least I can do." She gives me another bubbly grin, then checks her watch. "Okay, got to run. Great meeting you again, Emilia." She looks to Smith. "I'll let Macie know you loved her card."

His scowl deepens, and she laughs, giving us a wave before hustling to her car.

"I like her," I say, watching her go. "She seems fun."

"She is. She was super shy when I first started coming here, and it took a while for her to warm up to me. We're good now though."

I kind of picked up on that when Miller was here. There wasn't a lot of eye contact, and I swear her hand was shaking as she gave him his coffee.

"Do the other guys come here often?"

He nods. "Yeah, but don't tell your uncle or anyone. We'll get in trouble for eating too many donuts during the season."

I slide my eyes over him, trying not to pay too close attention to the way his simple gray t-shirt clings to his muscles. "I think you'll be just fine."

"Stop checking me out, Ms. Anderson. We're here to work. This isn't a *date*."

There's a bite to the last word, and I wonder if I offended him by being so quick to correct Scout about our relationship status. It's just that if the other players are coming here often, the last thing I need is for her to say something to one of them about Smith and me and have it get passed around the locker room. That's how rumors start. That's how we get memos sent out.

That's how people lose their jobs.

And by actually breaking the rules.

I shove down the thought, locking it tightly away in a box and pushing it to the depths of my mind.

"Speaking of work…"

I pull a small travel-sized tripod from my bag and set it up, getting my phone ready to make some short videos we can use across a few different platforms. Then I pluck my tablet from my bag, clearing text notifications from Blake and pulling up the questionnaire we've been slowly working our way through over the past month. I scroll to find where we left off last.

"All right, so we left off with…" My voice trails off when I realize Smith is staring at me, head tipped to the side, mouth set in a firm line. "What? Do I have something on my face?" I reach up to check but find nothing.

He shakes his head. "No."

"Then what is it?"

"It's…" Another headshake. "Nothing."

But it's not nothing. I *know* it's not nothing.

He's thinking about the same things I am, and I'm starting to wonder just how much longer we're going to be able to keep our bubble alive.

He clears his throat, shifting on the bench. "So, where'd we leave off?"

"This question is from Kaden, age five," I tell him, reading off the list. "If you were a dinosaur, what kind would you be, and why would it be a T-rex?"

Smith laughs. "Hard-hitting questions. I like it. So, I'd be…" He dives into a very detailed explanation of his answer, and I love that he takes it seriously.

We spend the next half hour going through the rapid-fire questions, getting a good number of videos saved so we can spread them out and post them over the next several weeks. Tori has been pleased with everything

I've gotten Smith to agree to so far. She has no idea it's because I've been promising him blow jobs in exchange for content.

"All right," I say once we reach the end of the list. "I think that's good for today."

"Yeah?" Smith rises from the table, stretching. "Does this mean you're off the rest of the day?"

"Uh, no." I laugh at the way he bounces his brows up and down and start packing up my things. "I have to go back to the office and start editing these, and *you* need to take a pre-game nap, Mr. Hockey Star."

"We can nap together?" he tries, coming around the table to wrap an arm around my waist and tug me close.

I hate the way my eyes scan the lot, making sure nobody is watching. Thankfully, the place is totally empty now, and aside from Scout's sister in the truck, we're alone. I sag against him, letting him press soft kisses into my neck.

"Come on. Naps are way more fun with you."

"That's because we don't nap!"

"True."

He presses against me harder, and there is no mistaking the erection I feel against my ass. He nips at my neck, then runs his tongue over the same spot, licking away the sting from his bite. I tug my lip between my teeth, trying to fight the moan that's threatening its way up my throat.

"It's not my fault," he says into my ear, his fingers dangerously close to slipping under my skirt. "You taste too good." He grinds against me again. "There's always now."

"Hmm?"

"If you won't come home with me, there's always now. My truck is pretty big, you know…"

I groan at the thought of straddling Smith in the back seat, riding him until we're both exhausted.

"Emilia…"

A vehicle with music thumping loudly races into the parking lot, and it's enough to pull me from my stupor. I wiggle out of his hold, and he lets me go easily, not-so-subtly adjusting the bulge in his pants. I clear my throat, pressing out the wrinkles in my clothes, then finish packing up my things.

We throw our trash away, and Smith's hand finds the small of my back again as we make our way to his truck. It's a simple touch, a thoughtless one, but it's still making my skin burn beneath his fingertips, and I wonder if it'll always feel that way with him, if he'll always make me feel like I'm constantly on the edge of something great.

He pulls the door open for me, helping me into the passenger seat.

"Smith?" I say, just before he's about to close the door.

"Yes?"

"Ten minutes, but that's it."

He grins. "I only need nine."

CHAPTER 20

"I'm sorry, but no. The remakes are better."

I blink at her. "Oh, you poor, sweet, summer child. *Jumanji* is a classic."

"Listen here, *old man*, just because it came from the eighties, doesn't mean it's better."

"It's not even from the eighties! It was released in 1995, and I remember that because I took Stephanie Martinez to the dollar theater to see it and we kissed."

A little growl escapes her when I mention that last bit, and I admit it brings me great satisfaction to see her jealous.

We had a home game tonight, which means Emilia is sleeping over. It's been that way for over a month now. She comes over and some nights we have dinner and talk, others we fuck, and some we just go straight to bed. I don't know exactly when it started, but we both seem to be content with not questioning it.

I'm too tired to cook after getting our asses handed to us by St. Louis, so we're currently lounging on the couch.

Emilia's popping French fries into her mouth while I slowly eat a chicken Caesar salad as Robin Williams' *Jumanji* plays in the background.

Even when she admits to having shitty taste in movies, I love having her here. It feels natural, normal—and a lot like that thing that's been missing for far too long.

"Godzilla!" she exclaims. "Puh-*lease* tell me you're at least team Godzilla and not rooting for Kong."

I shake my head. "I am so disappointed in you. There is no way. King Kong all the way. Hell, it's in his name—he is king."

"No." It's all she says as she chucks the fry at my head. What she forgets is that I'm a pro athlete and I have no problem snatching it out of the air. I pop it into my mouth, grinning at her when she glares at me.

"Yes," I say again.

She rolls her eyes. "You do realize there are scientists —*actual scientists!*—out there who agree that Godzilla would whoop that ass, right?"

"How do you know that?"

She shrugs. "I read the internet."

"Yes, and the internet is never wrong."

"Was it wrong about your butt?"

"What about my ass?"

"There's an Instagram account—*HockeysBestButts*—and all they do is talk about hockey butts. Every year they do a playoff-bracket-style head-to-head battle with a bunch of polls to determine who has the best butt. This year, you won. Well, your butt won."

"*My* ass won?" She nods. "From the entire league?"

"Yep. It was down to you and Elias Hasselback from Vancouver. It was close, but you squeaked out just ahead."

"I...don't even know what to say to that."

She laughs. "It's a compliment, trust me. Harper said Collin was *very* upset that you beat him in the semifinals."

"Well, that would explain the looks he's been sending me for the last week. I'm totally going to give him shit for following the poll."

"Apparently he was checking it obsessively. Make sure to throw that in there too."

I point at her. "Now that is good ammo to have in my back pocket."

"You're welcome." She shimmies her shoulders, popping another fry into her mouth and tuning back into the movie.

But I don't. I watch her shamelessly, loving the way her face changes as the movie plays out. The way her eyes spark and dim, how her nostrils flare, and even when she huffs, annoyed at something in the plot.

It's crazy to me how well she fits into my life, how right this feels...how I could get really used to this if I let myself.

"You know I can feel you staring at me, right?"

"You know I don't care, right?"

She laughs. "Kind of figured." She stretches her

arms over her head as the credits of the movie roll across the screen. "Okay, so what's next?"

"Next is bed. It's late and I'm tired."

"It's not *that* late."

"Um, some of us are over thirty *and* played a hockey game today."

"Some of us are old and boring too."

I narrow my eyes at her. "You did not just call me old and boring."

She looks pointedly at the puzzle strewn across my living room table. I've picked the habit back up again, mostly due to Emilia's insistence, and it didn't take me long to realize I missed it. I missed how I could just shut my mind off and piece something together.

"Don't be hating on my puzzling, young lady."

"What are you going to tell me next? To get off your lawn?"

I glower. She laughs.

But her laughter is gone when I spring from my end of the couch and dart over, fitting my body over top of hers and pressing her into the cushions. I slide her hands above her head, gathering her wrists in one hand, holding them there.

"Are you looking to start something?" I ask, rolling my hips into hers, letting her feel the erection growing beneath my sweats. She does that to me, makes me hard and ready all the fucking time.

I know she joked about my refractory time, but with her, it's never an issue. My body craves hers every minute of every day, and I can't seem to get enough. Hell, I don't know if I ever will.

"Possibly," she admits, biting down on her lower lip.

"You're insatiable, you know that?"

"Only when it comes to you."

I grin, leaning down to press soft kisses against her neck. She sighs when my lips meet her skin.

"That was a good answer," I say against her.

"I know. Do you think it's earned me a reward?"

I laugh. "Insatiable."

"Mhmm," she agrees, arching up into me, seeking the friction I'm just as eager to provide.

For a moment, I wonder if I'll ever tire of this—tire of being near her, kissing her, feeling her beneath me.

I decide right then that, no, I won't, and somehow, that thought isn't as scary as it should be.

I thrust against her again. "Do you want me to fuck you, Emilia?"

"I thought you'd never ask."

She sighs when I nip at her neck, careful not to bite too hard so I don't leave any marks, her hips meeting mine in sync.

"But, Smith?"

"Hmm?" I say into her.

"I call top this time."

And I let her have it.

"Yo, Smith, your girlfriend is here."

My head snaps up at Miller's words just in time for him to step out of the way and see Emilia standing behind him.

"Shut up, Miller," she mumbles, and I laugh at her uncharacteristic act of unprofessionalism. She shakes her phone my way. "I'm just here for content."

"Again?"

She rolls her eyes, and it physically makes my hand twitch with the urge to walk over there and smack her ass for the gesture. "Yes, again."

"Here?"

She knows what I'm really asking. *Are we going to be alone, or will there be an audience?*

"Wherever you're most comfortable."

I glance around at the guys sitting at the table. Rhodes' face is buried in his lunch, Wright's focused on his phone, Miller is staring off into space, and Lowell is nowhere to be found.

Nobody is paying a lick of attention to us, but I still don't want to be around them.

I want to be alone with Emilia.

"All right. I'll meet you at the truck in five."

She tries to hide her grin, but I still see the corners of her lips twitch just before she turns and struts away.

Against my better judgment, I watch.

And apparently, I'm wrong about nobody paying any attention because Miller says, "I saw that."

I glance over at him. "Saw what?"

"Your eyes on her ass."

I narrow my eyes at him, then shrug it off. "It's a nice ass."

"Yeah, but you're like a gentleman and shit. You don't look at women's asses."

He's so fucking wrong that it's almost funny.

I'm no gentleman. Especially not where Emilia's concerned.

"Shut up, Miller," I echo her earlier words, rising from the table.

I grab my trash from my lunch and toss it, then dump my plate with our kitchen staff.

"In a hurry?" Greer asks, stepping up next to me as I quickly scrape my leftovers into the trash. "I saw that hot piece of ass head out of here. Meeting her for a quickie in the parking lot?"

I want to knock his fucking teeth in for talking about Emilia like that, but I know retaliation will be more telling than not.

"We're just working on that stupid player profile."

"Right. Sure. Keep telling yourself that."

"Fuck off, Greer."

He laughs, but I ignore him.

I try to keep my steps steady and unhurried as I make my way toward the parking lot.

I'm annoyed with Greer, but my frustration melts away the moment I see her waiting at my truck, and I can't help the grin that stretches across my face.

She's leaning against it and—a rare occasion for sure

—her red hair is blowing in the wind. Her toned legs mirror her crossed arms as she waits.

She's peering down at her phone with her brows pinched together in concentration, her bottom lip tucked between her teeth, something I've come to notice that she does often when she's really focused.

Her head lifts when she hears me approaching and that grin that teased her lips in the dining hall comes back full force when she spots me.

I don't stop. Not until I'm crowding her against the truck.

"Hi," I say, pressing into her.

"Hi." She looks left, then right. "You do know we're in public, right?"

Shit. I forgot.

"I know. I'm just getting your door." I reach around her and pop open the passenger door.

"Smooth," she says, ducking under my arm and climbing into the truck.

"I know we're in public, but am I allowed to tell you that your ass looks incredible in those pants?"

She laughs. "I'll allow it."

I jog around to the driver's side and hop in. I fire up the engine, then pull out with a little more gumption than I typically do.

Neither of us speaks.

Not until I swing into a random parking lot just half a mile down the road.

"What are you—"

I don't even bother whipping into a spot. I just throw the truck into park and lean across the center console, pulling her to me and pressing my lips to hers.

She sighs against me the moment our lips meet like she's been waiting for this all day too. Never mind that I just saw her this morning when she was leaving my bed at six AM. It feels like it's been years since I've touched her rather than hours.

I have no idea how long we kiss. It could be only seconds, or it could be thirty minutes. I just know when we part, we're both gasping for air.

"Is it too soon to say I missed that?" she asks.

"Only if I can say it too."

She grins. "Do you mind if we stop by my apartment? I want to grab different shoes. My feet are killing me today."

"You want to go to your apartment?"

"If that's okay?"

"Of course," I tell her, putting the truck back into drive and pulling from the lot.

I know the general area she lives in but I've yet to go to her place. This will be my first time and I'm anxious to see it.

She directs me to her place—which isn't too far from the rink—and I find a spot to park out front.

Hand on the door, she turns to me and says, "No funny business. We're just here for shoes."

I hold my hands up innocently. "Wasn't even thinking about it."

That's a lie.

I totally was.

I follow her up three flights—very much enjoying the view—then wait patiently as she unlocks her door.

"It's not much," she warns unnecessarily as she pushes inside.

We step into the place she's been spending a lot less time and she's right, it's not much. But it's hers, which makes me automatically love it.

That and the distinct hint of lavender that I can smell at every turn.

The first thing I notice is how different it is from my place. I'll admit that my apartment is decorated like a museum with very, *very* little décor, but not Emilia's. There are touches of her around every square inch of the place. From the vintage typography posters hanging on the wall to the pictures of her and Hollis attached to a corkboard, to the bookshelf that's overflowing with romance novels. It's exactly what I pictured when I thought of her.

"I'll be right back," she says, peeling her heels off, then darting down the hall.

I follow her, watching as she slides open the door to her closet and drops to her knees as she begins rifling around her shoes.

I'd be lying if I said naughty thoughts didn't filter through my mind the moment her knees touched the carpet.

But I push them aside.

Since she has no interest in showing me the comfort of her bed, I help myself.

She turns when she hears me flop down and narrows her eyes.

"I thought I said no funny business."

"I'm not here for funny business." I bounce up and down on the bed a few times. "Just testing it out. For the future."

"Uh-huh." She still sounds like she doesn't believe me, not that I blame her.

"I promise. I have a game tonight. I have to preserve my energy."

She shoves to her feet. "I suppose that's fair."

"Wait. Are you disappointed that I'm not trying to hit on you?"

She lifts her shoulders. "Maybe a little."

I laugh. "Like I said, insatiable." I pat the spot beside me. "Come. Lie down."

She eyes me skeptically.

"I meant what I said. No fooling around. Not right now." I wink and she shakes her head with a smile.

But she doesn't argue anymore. She hops up onto her bed, lying down.

"What are you…"

Her words die when I lift her feet into my lap and begin massaging the right one.

She moans as I press my thumb into the middle.

"Oh god. That feels incredible."

"Why do you wear those heels if they hurt? I mean,

don't get me wrong, they're incredibly sexy. But if they're painful, why?"

She shrugs. "They make me feel powerful. Important."

"You don't need heels for that. You're already powerful and important."

Another grin plays on her lips. "I'm glad you think so."

"Know so," I argue, pressing deeper into the spot.

She moans again and I do my best to subtly adjust the growing erection in my shorts.

If she notices, she doesn't say anything. She just lies there and lets me massage her feet.

I have no idea how long I knead my thumbs into her feet.

No idea how long I watch her enjoy every single moment of it.

But however long it is, it's worth every single second just to see the pure bliss that's melting over her face.

I'd do anything she wanted to keep it there because seeing her happy and making her feel good makes *me* happy and feel good.

"You keep this up and I just might start to like you, Owen," she murmurs quietly.

"Yeah? Might be a little late for me in that department, Emilia."

She tucks her lips together like she's trying not to smile at that.

The craziest part? I mean it.

Wright passes the puck to Rhodes, who drags it around the back of our net and sends it up the boards to Lowell. We race into Minnesota's zone with numbers. Lowell dekes around two players, winds it up, and fires.

The puck goes wide, and I race to it, beating the Minnesota player, but he shoves me against the boards, battling for the free puck. I win it back, then swing it back over to Lowell, who takes another shot, and this time he scores.

This ties the game three to three, but twenty seconds later, Minnesota scores again, and it's a real fucking bummer for us, because the game is over just five seconds later.

"Fuck!" Lowell screams out, beating his stick against the boards as he heads down the tunnel.

He's upset, and I get it. I'm pissed too. There was no reason we shouldn't have walked out of this game with two points we desperately need. We were more rested. We were hungrier.

But in the end, it wasn't enough.

The race for the playoffs is tight, and we're sitting in a wild card spot now. We don't have many more games on the schedule to get our shit together, which is something we really need to do. We're sinking, and we're going down fast.

I plop down onto the dressing room bench, sucking in gulps of air as I try to catch my breath and mentally go over everything that went wrong in the game. If we can't get it together, this season is going to be over sooner than any of us want.

"That fucking sucked," Miller complains, dropping down next to me, his gear already halfway off.

I'm still fully dressed, too pissed to move just yet.

"Tell me about it," I grumble. "We keep this shit up and we're losing that wild card position."

He makes a noncommittal noise next to me, his brows drawn tight.

"It'd help if you caught a pass," Greer mutters. "Stopped daydreaming about a certain redhead."

It's said quietly, but I don't fucking miss it.

I flip him off. "Just like it'd help if we didn't have to play like there was nobody in our net."

He scowls, not liking the fact that he let in two soft goals when Minnesota caught him sleeping.

It's stupid to get into a battle with him about it because really, it was *all* of our faults that we lost. Miller could have taken more shots. Rhodes could have had more hits. And Lowell and Wright could have worked harder together.

Me? I could have stopped daydreaming about Emilia and what it would be like to just be open and free with her.

We all fucked up, and it blows because every lost game is another lost chance at *the* game. It's another game wasted in a season where I should be savoring them, not squandering it all.

There's a damn good chance this could be my last year in a Comets uniform. Hell, this could be my last year in *any* hockey uniform. I wanted to go out with a fight, but it's really beginning to look like I might not even get that chance, and I'm really not ready for that.

I'm not ready for a lot of things.

Especially not admitting that maybe—just maybe— I'm steadily falling for Emilia.

CHAPTER 21

Smith: Tell me again why I'm sitting on a bus next to Miller and not waking up next to you right now.

Emilia: Because you're getting paid millions of dollars.

Smith: Ah, right. That's it.

Emilia: And because for all you complain about him, you secretly love Miller.

Smith: No. Not even close.

Emilia: Keep telling yourself that.

. . .

Emilia: How did you end up drawing the short stick again?

Smith: Because I have shit-ass luck.

Smith: It happens all the time.

Smith: I'm starting to think it's rigged.

Emilia: You could be onto something there.

Emilia: I definitely wouldn't put it past Collin, that's for sure.

Emilia: Or maybe even Lowell.

Emilia: I still can't believe he and Hollis are going to be parents.

Smith: Tell me about it.

. . .

Smith: It feels like just yesterday he was strutting onto the ice and now he's having a kid.

Smith: Time flies too fast.

Emilia: Don't be so dramatic, old man.

Smith: I might be old but I'm not too old to bend you over my knee and spank your ass.

Emilia: Oooh is that a promise?!?!

Smith: Is that consent?

Emilia: Yes.

Emilia: I mean, I'm into it if you are.

Smith: Oh, Emilia. The things I'd like to do to you...

. . .

Emilia: Tell me them.

Smith: Did you miss the part where I'm sitting next to Miller?

Emilia: So?

Emilia: Hold your phone away.

Smith: I'd rather not get a boner sitting next to him.

Emilia: Please, Owen.

Emilia: I miss you.

Smith: I'd lay you down and spread those gorgeous legs of yours so I can get a look at your pretty pussy.

Smith: Then, I'd devour you. Eat at you like a starved man until you're begging for me to let you come.

. . .

Smith: But I wouldn't.

Emilia: That's just mean.

Smith: As mean as this is right now?

Smith: My fucking cock is rock hard, and Miller just asked why I put my jacket over my lap.

Emilia: What do I have to do to come?

Smith: That's easy. You'll let me fuck your throat.

Emilia: God yes.

Smith: I'll watch your pretty mouth stretch around my cock until tears are streaming down your face. And only after I fill your pretty mouth with my cum, I'll flip you onto your back and sink into you.

Smith: But only for a moment.

. . .

Emilia: WHAT?

Emilia: WHY?

Smith: Because I have more plans for you, Emilia.

Smith: Like watching your tight little asshole take my cock while I fuck your pussy with a dildo.

Smith: Like watching your ass cheeks turn red from the sting of my palm.

Smith: Like watching you beg for mercy.

Smith: There's so much more I want to do to you, but it's getting really uncomfortable sitting here.

Emilia: Yes. Please. Now.

. . .

Emilia: I want it all.

Smith: Me too, baby. Me too.

Smith: Great. We just pulled into the rink and my dick won't go down.

Emilia: Oopsie?

Smith: Thanks for the blue balls.

Emilia: *grins* You're welcome.

Smith: What are you wearing?

Emilia: Uh, khakis.

Smith: Are you even old enough to know that commercial?

. . .

Emilia: Everyone knows Jake from State Farm!

Smith: Okay, that's fair.

Smith: But seriously…what are you wearing?

Emilia: Wouldn't you like to know?

Emilia: (Also, it really is khakis.)

Smith: Is it bad if I say that's hot?

Emilia: You're totally picturing my ass right now, aren't you?

Smith: Guilty.

Emilia: Your goal was so beautiful!

. . .

Smith: Eh. That was all Lowell on the setup. I just got lucky.

Emilia: Hush and take the compliment, Smith.

Smith: Yes, ma'am.

Emilia: Oooh, you're right. That IS nice.

Smith: You finished?

Emilia: Not yet, but if you give me a few minutes, I'm sure I can get there.

Emilia: ATTACHMENT

Emilia: All right, fine, it was less than a few minutes.

Smith: Fuck. Did you really just masturbate?

. . .

Emilia: I think the gleaming vibrator says it all, don't you?

Smith: I've never wanted to wish hockey games away so damn badly before.

Emilia: Don't. You need the points.

Smith: Don't try to talk sense into me now.

Smith: Also, I kind of hate you right now. We're still on the bus back to the hotel, and my cock is rock hard. There's no way I can stand up without everyone seeing it.

Emilia: I'm not even a little sorry.

Smith: You think you're so cute being so sassy when you're so far away.

Smith: Just remember that payback is a bitch.

. . .

Emilia: And I can't wait to meet her.

Emilia: Last game of the road trip. You guys got this.

Smith: If I score, do I get to see your titties?

Emilia: Just one.

Smith: Which one?

Emilia: Goal-scorer's choice.

Smith: The left. It's my favorite.

Emilia: What's wrong with the right one??

Smith: Nothing. The left one is just slightly bigger.

Emilia: It is, isn't it?

. . .

Emilia: That's the dominant tit.

Smith: You can have a dominant tit?

Emilia: Yes.

Emilia: It's a girl thing. Trust me.

Smith: I'll go ahead and believe you on that one.

Emilia: You should.

Emilia: Now go kick some ass for the titties.

Smith: *titty

Emilia: *dominant titty

CHAPTER 22

Six hours.

That's how long I have to go until I get to see Smith again. The Comets have been on a four-game road trip, and going so many days without seeing Smith feels wrong.

I miss him.

I know I shouldn't because getting attached to him is a horrible idea, but I can't help it. Spending time with him is quickly becoming my favorite thing to do. It's not just the sex either—though that is incredible. It's more than that. It's the nights we spend curled on the couch watching a movie, or the times when I'll read while he does recovery on his quads with the massage gun. And, okay, fine, it's also the nights when he strips me bare and makes me beg for mercy.

Even though I'm more swamped than ever with work, I can't remember a time when I've been this content. I feel good, *happy*, and there is absolutely no denying that it's all because of Smith.

I wish I could bottle this feeling and keep it forever, especially since I know that as long as he's playing for the Comets and I'm working for them, it can never last.

Hollis' idea of *who has to know* works for now, but I know we'll never be fortunate for it to last forever.

For now, I'm going to keep shoving down all the ways I know this is wrong and enjoy all the right ones while our time bomb keeps ticking away.

"Emilia!"

My head snaps up at Tori's abrupt entrance. "Yes?"

"My office. Five minutes."

Her words are short and clipped, but they always are. Her face is giving nothing away either; it's almost like she's bored.

But I know that's not the case. The way her eyes are locked on me...something is off, something I can't quite place my finger on, but whatever it is, I know I don't like it.

I nod. "Okay."

She tips her head, studying me. Then with a final nod, she disappears down the hall.

I swallow back the dread that begins to work its way up my throat and hit save on the posts I'm drafting. I rise from my desk, not missing the way my legs wobble, and take a deep breath.

Does she know about Smith? Is that what this is? Am I getting fired?

No, no, no. There's no way for her to know. We've been careful, professional every minute we're at work.

271

Not a single slip up while we're on the clock. If she knows, she's damn good at reading people.

Still…I'm nervous.

Tick.

I take a tentative step toward her office, then another. Several other staff members are looking my way, some sending sympathetic smiles, and I wonder for a moment if they can hear my heart trying to beat out of my chest. If they can hear the hitch in my breath. If they know something I don't.

"Psst!" I peek over my shoulder to find Blake poking his head out from the break room. "What's going on?"

I shrug. "No clue."

His eyes dart toward Tori's office, then back to me, and I hate the terror I see in his eyes. "She seems off."

Great—it's not just me picking up on that.

"Good luck," he says, and I can see the sympathy and worry in his eyes. I don't like that either.

Slowly, I continue to Tori's office, making sure not to rush but also not taking too much time. Somehow, I know I'm already walking a fine line, and I'd rather not make whatever this is any worse.

Tick.

"Close the door," Tori says calmly when I step into her office, not bothering to look up at me.

I press the heavy door closed, then take a seat opposite her. She continues scribbling something while I try to hide the way my hands are shaking. I fold them into my lap, hoping she doesn't catch it.

Only then does she set her pen aside and meet my eyes.

"Do you know why I asked you in here?"

To fire me. "Um...no?"

It comes out as a question, and by the lift of her brow, I know she doesn't like it.

"As of the end of April, I will no longer work for the Comets organization. I'll be going to the board on Monday to inform them of the decision as well as to officially nominate you for the open director position."

Relief floods me, not just because this isn't about Smith and me, but because *I got it.* It's not official yet since the board has to approve it, sure, but with Tori's recommendation, it's nearly a sure thing.

"However, there is something we need to address."

Tick.

I swallow.

She opens a drawer on her desk and pulls out a tablet. She sets it on her desk, then folds her hands together, setting a sharp gaze on me.

"Is there anything you'd like for me to know, Emilia?"

Yes. I'm sleeping with Smith. I'm breaking rules. I'm not the dutiful employee you think I am.

I *should* say all of that. I know that.

But...I don't.

Instead, I push my shoulders back and I tell her, "No."

The corners of her mouth pull down at my answer, and she sighs. "All right, then."

She turns the tablet on, then swipes a few times before flipping it my way and setting it in front of me. She dips her head toward it, but I don't look.

I can't.

Because I have a feeling that whatever she's showing me is evidence. And it's damning.

"You forgot to log out."

BOOM!

My whole world explodes.

I close my eyes, trying to will away the tears that are stinging and threatening to spill.

"How long?" she asks quietly.

"Over two years."

She sucks in a sharp breath, and I finally peel my eyes open.

"I met him when I moved here. It was just a one-time thing. We didn't exchange last names or talk about our jobs. When the next season rolled around…" I trail off, remembering that crushing feeling when our eyes caught across the room for the first time in months. "We didn't know, I swear, and when we realized it, we didn't have any contact outside of work and kept our contact *at* work to a minimum. I always had Blake cover anything to do with him until…"

"The player profile."

I nod. "Until then."

She twists her lips together, studying me as she drums her fingernails on the desk.

This is it for me. I know it is. I'm losing my job and

everything I've been working so hard for. My uncle is going to be so disappointed in me.

Hell, *I'm* disappointed in myself.

After what feels like hours of her just staring at me, finally, she sighs, leaning forward.

"You're an incredible asset to this team, Emilia, and I truly believe so much of our growth in the past year has been thanks to the fresh ideas you bring to the team."

I try hard not to let my mouth fall open. This is the nicest she's ever been to me, and I'm shocked. And I'm just as shocked to see nothing but compassion in her usually fiery gaze.

"What I'm about to say doesn't leave this room. Understood?"

I nod.

She clears her throat. "Maybe it's my pregnancy hormones talking or maybe it's because I know I'm not going to find anyone else to do this job as well as I have, but because of your dedication to this team and this organization, and because I truly do think you are the best replacement, I am willing to overlook this... transgression and give you the opportunity to stay. However, if you stay, you need to know whatever it is you have going on with Owen Smith is over. The board will not be as lenient and understanding as me."

This time, my jaw does drop, and I don't even bother trying to hide it. She's...giving me another chance? If it is her hormones, I don't care. I am not about to look a gift horse in the mouth.

"I—"

She holds her hand up, stopping me. "No. Don't say anything yet. Take a night. Think it over. Make sure this is what you truly want. What you're ready to give up. If it is, I'll go to the board on Monday with the recommendation."

I'm speechless. Part of me wants to scream at her that I don't need time to think about it. This is what I want.

But I can't get the words to come out, and I'm not sure why. Possibly because the idea of walking away from Smith again…it makes my stomach sink.

We knew this day was coming. This thing we've been doing, this bubble we've been living in…we knew it was temporary from the beginning.

Now, it's time to let it go.

Smith has been married to hockey his entire life. He knows what it's like to want to give something your all.

He'll understand.

He has to…right?

I've been sitting in my car outside Smith's apartment for nearly thirty minutes now. His game ended two hours ago, and by my calculations, he should have gotten to his apartment just before I pulled up, which means he should be upstairs waiting for me because that's what we do. That's our routine.

Funny, because we were never supposed to have any of those, but we do.

Did.

Yeah, I broke the rules and slept with a player. But my worst offense of all? I got attached. I got attached, and now I have to let him go.

I don't *want* to let him go.

There's a sharp knock on my window, and I jump at the sudden intrusion.

When my gaze focuses on what's in front of me, I realize it's Smith. He's staring down at me with his brows pinched tightly, head tipped to the side, probably completely confused as to why I'm just sitting in my car and not racing up to his apartment to crawl beneath his sheets.

It's because I'm scared.

I'm scared if I go up there, I won't be able to do it. I'm scared if I go up there, I'll want to stay. I'm scared if I go up there, I'm going to realize everything I'm giving up.

And more than all of those reasons, I'm scared because if I go up there, I just might realize I'm in love with him.

With a steadying breath, I step out of my tiny car. Smith holds open the door for me. He offers me a hand, but I decline it. I probably shouldn't be touching him. It's for the best.

I close the door, then rest against it, staring up at the building that holds so many memories for me.

Smith's been to my apartment a few times, but having him there never felt like it should. This place? This place feels right. It feels like home.

Or at least it used to.

He steps in front of me, his knuckles grazing under my chin as he tips my face up to his, those damn watchful ochre eyes of his boring into me and trying to find all my secrets.

I decide it's best to just rip the Band-Aid off.

"I talked with Tori today."

His nostrils flare, and it's the only indication that he heard me.

"I got the promotion."

He sighs with relief, much the same way I did in her office, then he presses his forehead against mine, his hand crashing into my hair like it always does.

"That's amazing, Emilia. I'm so proud of you."

His words are genuine. I can tell they are, and it makes my heart hurt even more.

"You deserve this. It's everything you've wanted. It's—"

"She knows, Smith." I pull back, meeting his eyes. "She knows about us."

"Ho…" He shakes his head. "How?"

"I connected my phone to a tablet at work. We do it all the time so we can get texts while we're working and not have to worry about carrying around multiple devices, and I…I didn't disconnect it. Which means…"

My words trail off, but he nods, understanding where I'm going.

"Our texts. She saw our texts."

"Everything. All of it. I'm so sorry."

I try so hard to fight back the tears that are so close to spilling free, but it's pointless. They fall anyway.

"Hey, shh. It's okay," he says, pressing a kiss to my forehead and then bending slightly to meet my eyes. "It's all right. I—"

"No." I shake my head. "You don't get it. It's not all right. I—"

I watch it happen in real time, the truth hitting him. First, his eyes darken, then his pupils dilate. His breaths change, coming in shorter, sharper. And finally, he drops his hold on me, putting entirely too much space between us.

"I'm choosing the job, Smith," I tell him quietly. "I have to."

He doesn't move. He doesn't even blink, and for a moment, I wonder if he heard me at all.

Then, he blows out a heavy breath. "Okay."

"Okay?" He nods, and it pisses me off for some reason. "Just *okay*?"

His eyes harden. "What do you want me to say, Emilia? You've already made up your mind. This is what you wanted from the beginning, and now you're getting it. I get it. I understand. I'm not some young guy who is going to go off the handle about this. I'm too old for dramatics. It's your job, and that's important. I understand."

I knew he would, but for some reason, I can't help but wish he were a little more upset about this, wish he cared more about losing me, wish he *wanted* to fight for me.

But I know his hands are tied. He's a professional hockey player under contract. Of course this was going to end like this. We always knew it would.

I just didn't think saying goodbye would hurt this badly.

"It was fun, though, right?"

I hate his flippant tone. Hate the way he's standing there stoic and unflinching. Like none of this hurts him. Like he's not feeling an ounce of the same heartache I am.

Was this all in my head? Did I build us up to be something more?

I want to tell myself it's just a coping mechanism and he's just trying to convince himself he doesn't care but deep down he really does.

But I'm not so sure.

All I know is that whatever bubble we've been hiding in, it's long gone.

And this time, it's for good.

When I walk into the arena, I shove my shoulders back and will myself not to cry.

I managed to get my tears to stop long enough this morning to apply my mascara and drive to work without wrecking. Hell, I didn't even cry until I pulled into the parking lot.

Now that I'm here and walking through these doors, I want to cry again.

Usually, I'm eager to come to work. I love my job.

But right now? Right now, I hate it.

I hate it *because* I love it, and because I love it, I went and got myself brokenhearted.

"Hey, kiddo. How's it going?"

I startle at the sudden voice of my uncle, surprised that when I glance to my right, he's walking right next to me.

Was I so stuck in my head that I didn't hear him walking up?

"Good morning, Mr. Martin," I tell him.

He frowns. "What'd I tell you about calling me that? It's..."

"Professional?" I counter with a grin.

"Weird. I understand calling the players by their last names, but not your uncle."

The smile on my face falls when he mentions the players because my mind automatically goes to Smith.

Smith and the way his eyes changed right in front of me last night. Smith and the way he let me walk away.

Smith and the way my heart broke leaving him there.

281

"Oh. What was that look for?"

"What look?"

"The frown that just popped up out of nowhere."

"I didn't frown."

Uncle Jared places his hand on my arm, pulling me to a stop. His sharp eyes bore into me, and I hate how his stare penetrates the shield I've tried to construct.

He knows something is wrong.

Then his eyes flash wide, and he grabs my arm, hauling me off to the side of the hall, his brows tightly together.

He bends his head near mine, eyes dark and angry. "Did one of my players do something to you? Did they hurt you?"

"What?" It comes out a squeak. "No! God, no. It's not that."

I mean, it is. But not in the way he's thinking. And really, did *he* hurt me? Or did *I* hurt myself? I knew getting involved with Smith was a bad idea from the start. I set myself up for this heartbreak.

"Are you sure? Because I swear to god, Emilia, I'll—"

"No," I cut him off. "It's…no. Nobody did anything to me, Uncle Jared. It's fine. *I'm* fine."

Now he's the one frowning. "I don't like you lying to me, kiddo."

I can't help but grin because *of course* he knows I'm lying to him. He's been my rock for most of my life. He can sense it.

"I got the promotion," I tell him. "I'm on my way to tell Tori right now that I accept it."

"What?" The biggest smile I've ever seen replaces his frown. "That's fantastic! You deserve it!"

"I know." I nod, agreeing with him because I *do* deserve it.

His smile falters, and it's always funny to see him slip into protective parent mode when he's not technically my parent.

"You don't look happy about it. Why not?"

"It's just…" I blow out a breath. "I'm going to have to give up a lot for it."

"Your free time?" He laughs lightly. "Tell me about it. Working for an NHL team is no joke. But I know you can handle it. If you want to, of course."

I swallow the lump that's been forming in my throat.

He doesn't miss it.

"*Do* you want to?"

"Yes!" Another loud squeak. I clear my throat. "Yes," I say again quietly. I nibble on my bottom lip, trying to figure out the best way to talk to him about this without spilling my secret. *Smith's* secret. "Of course I want to. It's just…if I take this job, things will have to…change."

His brows are back to the same concerned position as before as he processes my words. "I'm not entirely sure I'm following."

I think I'm falling for your player.

I think I'm falling for your player, and I have no business falling for him.

I want so badly to confess everything to him, but I'm not sure I'm ready for his *I'm not mad, just disappointed* look I know I'll get.

So, I don't tell him.

"I think I'm just being silly." I wave my hand flippantly. "Nerves, you know? Big changes and all that."

He tips his head to the side, watching me. All I can do is pray he believes it and lets it go because I genuinely don't know much longer I can stand here and not fall apart in front of him. Especially if he keeps looking at me like he is.

Slowly, he straightens his head, then exhales heavily.

"I'm going to give it to you straight, all right?" I nod. "It's not going to be easy. In fact, it will probably really suck for a while. But it *will* get better. One day, you'll wake up, and everything with just be easier. It won't feel so heavy. It'll be like it was before. If anyone can endure this, it's you."

His words strike me in the chest like a missile hitting its target.

I know he thinks this is still about the promotion but his words… His words work on a level he's not even aware of.

And they are everything I needed to hear.

"You're strong, kiddo. Stronger than you give yourself credit for. You've got this."

His confidence in me astounds me, because it reminds me of the same faith Smith has in me. And everything hurts all over again.

But of course I can't tell him that.

Instead, I give him the best grin I can muster and say, "Thanks, Uncle Jared. I...I needed that pep talk. I'm going to talk with Tori."

"I think that's a good idea. Maybe dinner one night this week?"

"Sure." I give him another wobbly grin, then step around him, heading for the elevators.

I'm several feet away when he calls my name again.

"Yeah?" I ask, turning back.

"I'm always here for you, kiddo. Always. No matter what."

There's something in his words that makes me think he might understand more of what's going on than I think.

That's not possible, though, and I know that.

"Thanks," I mutter, and he nods.

I don't hang around, hustling toward the elevator at the fastest speed I can without making it look like I'm running away, which I am.

As luck would have it, the elevator is just a floor away, and I rush onto it faster than I ever before, letting out a long breath when the doors close and I'm alone.

I didn't like the way he was watching me. Like he just *knew* I was lying to him.

I really, really hate lying to him.

But what's the point in telling him now? The thing with Smith...it's done. We're done.

The car arrives on the social media floor as if it's a sign.

With a steadying breath, I exit the car and make my way to Tori's office, forcing my head up high as I rap my knuckles three times against the intimidating door in front of me.

"Come in!" I hear.

I push the door open and then walk inside Tori's office. I don't bother sitting down, choosing to stand.

This won't take long anyway.

When she realizes it's me standing there, she sits back, hand going to the bump protruding out of her belly, a reminder that soon she won't be here and it will be me sitting behind that desk.

"Well?" she says by way of greeting, clicking the pen in her hand several times, waiting eagerly for my answer.

I shove my shoulders back, tipping my chin up. "I'm in."

"Good. That's good." A grin curves her lips, and she looks incredibly satisfied by my choice. "Effective immediately, you're no longer working on the player profile. Blake will take over the project, and you will start shadowing me so we can make this transition as smooth as possible for all involved. Understood?"

I nod. "Yes."

"Excellent."

She ducks her head back down, returning to whatever it was she was working on before, and I know enough to understand that means our meeting is over. I head for the door, and just as I'm about to pull it open, she calls my name.

I spin around. "Yes?"

"For what it's worth, I think you're making the right decision."

I give her a tight smile and then close the door. I press my back against the wall just beside it, holding my hand to my chest, my heart feeling like it's about to leap out of my chest.

If it's the right decision, why does it feel so damn wrong?

CHAPTER 23

SMITH

She took the job.

She took the fucking job.

I knew it was coming all along, but it doesn't make it hurt any less.

I've tried hard to keep my feelings out of things because I knew from the start that at the end of the day, if I'm playing for the Comets, there's no way what we were doing was going to last. It would be a lot different too if I could actually be mad at her for taking the job. I can't be. She deserves it so much, and it would be easier if she didn't.

"Thanks for meeting with me," I say to Lowell as we park our asses on a picnic table.

"You look like ass," Lowell says in greeting as I sit down across from him. "And that's saying something coming from the guy with a newborn at home."

It's been a week since I've seen Emilia, and a lot has changed in that time. For starters, Hollis and Lowell had their baby, and she's perfect.

Second, Emilia is no longer spearheading the player profile. I've been working with Blake to wrap up all the social media posts and the final segments of the big interview that's set to air on our channels and local news stations in two weeks. With the playoffs—which we barely squeaked into—just a week away now, we're down to the wire on time, and I've admittedly been putting it off.

I like Blake. He's a cool dude.

But he's not Emilia.

I miss her. Her laugh, her smile, that fucking hair I love wrapping around my fist. I miss her sass and the way she confidently enters a room. I miss having her in my apartment and having her scent on my sheets. I miss her eyes and the way she screams my name.

I miss everything about her, and I have no fucking clue if I'll ever stop.

This wasn't supposed to mean anything. Just like that first weekend we had together wasn't supposed to mean anything.

But it did.

It *does*.

And I have no clue how to cope with that.

"This about her?" Lowell asks as if he can read my thoughts.

I want to ask him who *her* is.

But that would be insulting.

Lowell isn't stupid. He sees the way I look at Emilia.

I sigh, then nod. "Yeah."

He opens his box of donuts and then offers me one. I shake my head. I've not had the appetite for much lately, but I really can't stand the sight of the chocolate cherry donut he's offering me right now. It reminds me too much of her.

"I figured." He takes a sip of his coffee. "All right, let's hear it. Start from the beginning."

So, I do. I tell him everything from meeting Emilia the summer we lost the Cup to her promotion to breaking all the rules and Christmas and everything that came after that.

He listens, giving nothing away if he's surprised by any of it. When I'm done, he just sits there, staring at me.

And still staring.

Still. Fucking. Staring.

Finally, I snap. "What?"

He laughs. That motherfucker laughs.

"Dude," he says, shaking his head, "you are so damn in love with her it's ridiculous."

"You fucking think?" I grumble.

I know I'm in love with her. That's not that difficult to figure out, not with the way she makes me feel.

It's the being with her part that I can't seem to nail down.

"You know this is the dumbest thing you've ever done, right?"

"I'm…aware."

"She's Coach Martin's niece."

"I know."

"She works for the Comets."

I grit my teeth together, annoyed with him stating the obvious for a second time. "I know."

"She's the best friend of the woman I just had a child with. Of the woman I *love*."

"*I know.* What the fuck is your point?"

He shrugs. "Just letting you know you're dumb as shit."

I groan because he's not wrong. "I know."

He laughs lightly, even though there's not really any humor to it.

He knows this isn't the best situation for me to be in. He knows I'm screwed.

"Why didn't you tell me?"

I shrug. "You said it yourself. Who she is in relation to the team. To Coach Martin. To Hollis. It wasn't...ideal. Plus, you've had your own shit going on with the baby."

He nods. "Yeah, that's fair, I guess. But I'm always here, you know?"

"Yeah," I say, looking out at the mostly empty parking lot, watching Scout clean off the tables. She left us to ourselves this morning, almost like she knows we need the space.

I know Lowell is always there for me. But I also understand that this whole mess is something I got myself into—no sense in dragging him into it too.

"Look," he says after several minutes of silence and one donut. I turn my attention back to him. "I'm going to tell you something you're not going to like, okay?"

"On a scale of one to punching you, how much am I not going to like it?"

"Probably about a five. No—a six. Maybe seven. We'll see."

I motion for him to continue.

"You put your life on hold for hockey, right? The game has been your mistress for as long as you can remember. It's *all* your life has been, but now that game you love so much is turning its back on you. It's getting faster, and the competition is getting younger, fresher. It's pushing you away and you're trying to hold on to it for dear life, squeezing everything you can from it. But..." He shrugs. "Maybe you shouldn't. Maybe it's time for you to be done."

His words hit hard, because they're everything I've been stuffing down, too afraid to face.

"You said if I had a chance at a family and at love, I should lay my heart on the line and take it," he continues. "Well, maybe you should too. Maybe you should stop holding on to something that doesn't love you the same way it used to. Take a chance on something new—on *someone* new."

I hear what he's saying. I really do.

But it's hard, and fucking terrifying if I'm being honest. Giving up hockey would be like giving up breathing—it's impossible to do. The game is my oxygen, and I need it to live. Even if I did somehow find a way, the fact is, at the end of the day, that doesn't change the reality that Emilia chose the job and not me.

"She picked the job though," I say.

He shakes his head. "I thought you were supposed to be older and wiser."

I narrow my eyes at him.

He's unfazed. "Just because she didn't choose you, Smith, doesn't mean you can't choose her."

Choose her.

It seems like such a simple thing but feels so damn big and scary at the same time.

He drains his coffee and then rises from the bench. "Look, I have to get back home to my baby, but I'm going to tell you the same thing you told me: tell her. Tell her you love her. Tell her you wanted her to choose you. Then, choose her."

"Want to know what's bullshit?"

I glance up from the book I'm currently reading—I don't know what it is, something random I picked up yesterday at the store down the block from the hotel— just in time to see Coach Martin flop down into the empty seat next to me.

It's brave of him considering I've been in such a shit mood lately that not even Miller wanted to sit next to me today. I take pride in that defeat.

It's early morning, and we're on a bus in Philly heading to the rink for practice. It's quiet, and nearly everyone is still half asleep. We're not typically the chitchatting type, but here Coach is, in front of me with a grin, clearly fishing for conversation.

So, I bite.

"What's that, Coach?"

"Rules."

I was already on edge from losing the game last night, but that singular word has my heart hammering in my chest so loudly that I'm almost sure he can hear it.

Rules? Like the ones I broke by falling for his niece?

Like the ones I'd happily break again and again if it meant having Emilia back?

Because, yeah, those rules *are* bullshit.

I close the book, clearing my throat and shifting around until I sit up straighter. "Rules?"

He nods. "Yep. That offside rule screwed us last night, huh? You had that entire team beat. The goalie too. But…rules."

Oh. That's what he's referring to.

"Yeah, kind of brought down the whole team."

"Don't get me wrong here. I understand the offsides rule and why it's necessary. But sometimes a guy on the ice makes a play that's so damn beautiful and dangles around half a team to score, only for the goal to get called back. Bullshit, right?"

Considering I've been on both sides of that rule, I can agree. "Bullshit for sure, Coach."

"Mhmm." He nods, glancing around the bus at the other players.

Collin has his phone up to his ear, talking softly to

Harper, I'm sure. Lowell is on a video chat with Hollis and the baby, though nobody is talking. He's just staring at his sleeping daughter. And Rhodes is glaring at Miller, looking about two seconds away from strangling the idiot who is rambling on about something animatedly like he's not about to get murdered.

Everyone else is either buried in their phone or sleeping.

After several minutes, Coach looks back my way. "Say, how's the player profile going? I heard Blake is taking over for Emilia since she got promoted."

Emilia.

I've tried hard not to think about her, but I've failed at every attempt. I can't get her out of my mind. Not even when we're out on the ice, which is probably why I went in offsides last night and caused a nearly ten-minute delay while they reviewed it.

It was painful to sit through, but not nearly as painful as knowing that whatever I had with Emilia is done.

I rub at my chest when the truth of that hits me again.

He doesn't miss the gesture.

"He did," I answer. "It's going well. Almost finished."

"Good. That's good. We need you focused for the Playoffs anyway. It was nice having her around, though, wasn't it? She's one of the good ones."

One of the good ones? She's the fucking *best* one.

"Yeah," I agree. "She is."

"I love seeing her happy, and her work makes her happy."

It does. It makes her so damn happy, and while I love that for her, I hate it for me. For us.

"You remind me of her sometimes, you know?"

My brows crush together. "I do?"

"Yeah. Or maybe she reminds me of you." He shrugs. "Either way, you're similar. Always working hard and giving up so much for your jobs."

Guilty and guilty. I know we both give our all to this organization.

"Sometimes maybe a little too much," Coach says quietly.

I don't know if he's talking about Emilia or me or both of us. Either way, his words ring true. We've both chosen our jobs time and time again. Maybe a little too often like he suggests.

"I've done that before too, you know. I chose my job often. Over things I had no business putting up for questioning, like time with Maxine."

He smiles, but it's filled with sadness from bringing up his late wife.

I'm familiar with it because it's the same smile I've given since I watched Emilia walk away. Sure, I didn't lose Emilia like he lost his wife, but she's still gone, and it still fucking hurts.

"If I could go back, I'd choose differently. I'd choose her."

He says the last three words quietly, but I hear them the loudest.

Choose her.

His words hit me right in the chest because he's not the only one who has said them.

"Anyway," he says, pulling my attention back to him, "just thought I'd check-in and see how you're doing with…everything."

When I don't say anything right away, he laughs lightly.

"You know. The player profile and the game last night."

Right. *That* everything.

But I have a sneaking suspicion that we're not talking about the player profile or even offsides rules anymore.

Maybe we never were.

He nods to the book in my hand, a greenish cover with a golden swirl on top of a pair of legs. It's a weird cover for a weird book.

"You'll have to let me know your thoughts. If you're team letter or manuscript."

"Sure thing, Coach," I say, though I have no clue what he's talking about.

I watch as he stands and ambles his way to the back of the bus, leaving me alone with my thoughts.

What the hell was that? Does he know about Emilia and me? Was he just testing me? Or was he just making weird conversation?

I don't know.

All I know is that he is right about something.
Something that keeps hitting me in the face over and
over again.

Something I *need* to do.

I need to choose her.

And I think I know what I need to do for that to be
an option.

I don't let myself think about it as I rise to my feet
and make my way to the front of the bus.

"You mind if I sit here?"

Coach Heller looks up from his iPad, tugging his
reading glasses to the end of his nose. "Not at all."

"Thanks," I mutter, tossing myself into the seat next
to him. "Can I ask you something, Coach?"

"You can ask me anything—except a math question."
He grins. "I suck at math."

"How did you know it was time to hang up your
skates?"

His brows rise. "It was just one loss, Smith."

I don't grin back at him, and his smile slips from his
lips, the reality of what I'm asking him sinking in. It's
entirely too early to be having a serious conversation like
this, but I need to have it now before I chicken out.

He sighs. "I don't know. Sometimes it's slow and it
dawns on you over time. Sometimes it hits you out of
nowhere and you're just ready to be done. It's just a
feeling you get, something in your heart telling you it's
time."

"How did you know when to listen to it?"

"I'm not sure there's an answer for that. Some people never listen to it, and they just sort of fade away from the league but never the game."

I know what he means. There are guys out there who haven't ever officially retired but aren't in the NHL anymore. They're either playing abroad or hoping one day, somehow, a team will call them up again.

I don't want to be that guy. If I'm going to be done, I want to be done. I don't want there to be any questions left unanswered.

"Is there…something I should know, Smith?"

I shake my head. "No, Coach. Not yet."

"All right." He eyes me warily. "But if there is something on your mind, I'm here for anything."

"Unless it's math."

"Fucking hate math." He laughs heartily. "Look, kid, I'm not sure if this conversation has been much help, but I just want you to know I understand what you're going through. You'll figure it out. When it's time, you'll know. Just…give me a heads-up, yeah? I'll need to adjust the lines."

I laugh. "Sure thing, Coach."

"For what it's worth, I've seen you give your all to this game over the years. You've sacrificed a lot, and the game has taken too much time from you, controlled your life in a lot of ways because you let it—because it's easier that way." He gives me a knowing look. "Maybe it's about time you take back the reins."

I can't help but think of my conversation with Lowell.

About how he said I was holding onto the game that doesn't love me the way I love it.

Maybe they're on to something.

Maybe it *is* about time I took back the control, and I think I know just the way.

We pull into the rink, and the guys start piling off the bus. Coach gives me one last long look before following suit.

I pull my phone out of my pocket and tap the most recently added name on my contact list.

"Hello?"

"Blake," I say. "Do we still have time to film another piece?"

"Uh...yeah?" It comes out a question. "I mean, we really need to get things to editing, but if there's something you want to add, we can make it happen."

I'm scared to leave the game. Afraid to move on. I don't know who I am without hockey, and I don't even know if I will like that version of me.

But...part of me is ready to meet him.

Part of me is ready for something more.

And just maybe, that something more is Emilia.

"Good. I have an idea..."

CHAPTER 24

EMILIA

"I love my baby, I love my baby, I love my baby," Hollis chants over and over.

I try not to laugh as she tries not to gag at whatever it is baby Freddie—named after Freddie Mercury since she and Lowell are both in love with Queen—just did in her diaper. How something so little can make something so stinky, I have no idea.

Hollis forces a smile as she looks down at the awful-smelling newborn. "She's the greatest thing ever, and I love her *so* much." Freddie lets out a little yawn, and Hollis' smile isn't so forced anymore. "You're lucky you're cute, missy."

There's a tug at my chest watching Hollis with her daughter, and it makes me miss Smith all over again. Walking away from him was the hardest thing I've ever had to do, but no matter how much I miss him—and I *really* fucking miss him—it was the right thing.

The board approved Tori's motion to promote me,

and I'm the new Carolina Comets media relations director.

Me!

I still can't believe it. I can hardly think about what it took to get here, but it was just too big to say no to. It's what I've been busting my ass for over the last three years, right? I couldn't give up on it now, and certainly not because of some guy.

But...he's not just some guy, is he? He's more than that, and I'm afraid he always will be.

We haven't spoken since that night outside his apartment. Tori cut off all contact, having Blake step in for the profile and other staff members take over some of my old duties while she finished prepping me for the promotion.

I won't lie—at first, I regretted saying yes. Not just because my heart was threatening to burst out of my chest every time I stepped into the arena and had to see his face, but because the workload was massive. Tori wasn't kidding when she said I'd better be ready to sacrifice. Guess I got a lot more than I bargained for on several fronts there.

I rub at the ache that seems to permanently be in my chest.

Hollis doesn't miss it.

"Have you heard from him?" she asks, picking up Freddie and cuddling her to her chest once she's finished changing her diaper.

I shake my head. "No. Not since they pulled a Toronto and lost in the first round."

Her face scrunches up. "What does this have to do with Canada?"

I wave her off, sometimes forgetting she doesn't know hockey very well. "Nothing."

She shrugs. "Have you reached out to him at all?"

"No. I...I can't."

A frown tugs at her lips. "I get that." She narrows her eyes. "Don't think I'm not still mad at you, by the way."

I repress my sigh. "I know, and I'm still sorry."

"I just wish you would have confided in me." She adjusts Freddie, slipping her into a baby sling that's strapped to her chest. Freddie snuggles into her mom, a little grin on her lips.

"I wanted to. So badly, I really did. But with Lowell and you and everything else..." I lift my shoulders. "Well, I was kind of in a tough spot."

After the board approved the promotion, I told Hollis everything, the whole long, sordid tale.

Understandably, she was upset I kept it from her for so long, but she did say she suspected for a while that something might have happened between us.

"I know." She nods. "I understand." She tosses Freddie's diaper into the trash can and then pulls the bag out so my office doesn't start smelling. "Walk this down to the dumpster with me?"

With the Comets done for the season, there are not a lot of people bustling around the office. It's always weird having the place be so empty, but it doesn't stop me from still coming in.

Truthfully, I do it because if I don't, I'll have entirely too much time on my hands to think about things I shouldn't be. Today was going to be an off day, but Hollis asked if I could get her access to the arena because she wanted to take some photos with Freddie.

I jumped at the chance to spend time with them.

"Have you heard the rumors?" Hollis asks once we're in the elevator.

"You're going to have to be more specific. This is hockey—there are a lot of rumors in hockey."

"About him...about Smith."

I wince when she says his name like it physically hurts, and if the spot aching in my chest again is any indication, it does.

"No."

"They're talking retirement."

I snort out a laugh as the elevator descends. "Right. Sure."

Smith retire? Not yet. He sure as hell wasn't playing in the playoffs like he was planning to be done. He laid some heavy hits and got four assists and one goal before the team was eliminated. He was playing like he was ten years younger.

Besides, I'm the media relations director—I'd know if a player was retiring.

"Hmm" is all Hollis says.

We make our way from the elevators and through the

building, all the way around the concourse to the trash shoot, and dump it in.

"Did you want to set up any photos against the ice backdrop? Everything is still up and painted. We were doing some promo stuff in there yesterday, but it's getting torn out tomorrow."

She taps her fingers against her chin. "Actually, that doesn't sound like a bad idea. I could——"

There's a loud click that echoes throughout literally the entire building, then the sound of static fills the silence.

I look around the hall to see where it's coming from, and every single TV as far as I can see is on. Epic music begins to play, and the Comets logo flashes across the screen.

I give Hollis a *what the fuck is going on* look, and she just shrugs.

"No clue," she mutters.

The picture on the screen looks familiar, and it takes me a moment to recognize the makeshift set we use to do player interviews. There are soft footfalls, then a player walks into view, and I don't even have to see a clear picture to know who it is.

Smith.

The camera focuses as he takes a seat on the empty stool, and my chest aches at the sight of him.

"State your name and position," I hear my own voice say, and I know right away what's playing.

"My name is Owen Smith. My position is..." His

eyes drift just to the right and away from the camera.

God, I couldn't see it then, but I do now. The look he gives me is…

"Holy shit," Hollis mutters. "No wonder you banged him."

I laugh.

"Centerman," screen Smith says.

Then the commercial for this interview begins to play.

Even though I was there nearly every step of the way, I watch with rapt attention as clips and sound bites from the months-long profile we did with Smith fill the screen. There's video of him skating and setting his teammates up for a record number of assists, footage of him at Scout's Sweets and volunteering during our charity days. There are even a few clips of him cooking the crew breakfast at his apartment right after Christmas.

Despite his uncertainty being on camera, he looks incredible in every clip, and more than once I catch his eyes drifting away from the cameraman and to me.

"Here," Hollis murmurs, holding out a napkin for me.

I take it and dab at my eyes; I didn't even realize I was crying.

I'm crying for so many reasons. Because I'm so damn proud of him. Because I wish things were different.

Because I miss him.

Because I think I might love him.

The screen fades to black, and I look at Hollis again,

feeling a little ridiculous for crying but not seeing any judgment in her eyes.

"You okay?" she asks.

I nod. "I'll be fine. That was the commercial for his profile airing tomorrow. I don't know why it was playing now, but I was not expecting that."

"Yeah, that was weird. I—"

"Okay, seriously, Miller. Just stand there and be the cameraman." Smith's voice echoes around the empty hallways again.

My eyes jump back to the TVs, watching as someone —I assume Miller—skates backward, training a camera on a scowling Smith.

"I swear I'm going to punch you."

"Nope. You can't. You hurt me, and I'll sue for assault. I can do that now."

"This was a really bad idea," I hear Blake say somewhere off camera.

"Nah. It's going to look sick," Miller assures him, though he's dead-ass wrong.

If he means dizzying and awful, then yes, it will look "sick" for sure.

His hand appears in front of the camera.

"Three! Two! One! ACTION!" he shouts, his fingers miming the numbers.

When Smith just stands there, glaring, Miller sighs, dropping the camera to his side, and I hear Blake squeak, probably worried about the costly equipment I know he doesn't have permission to be using.

"Look, dude," Miller says, skating closer to Smith. "Don't just stand there looking like a dinosaur from *Jurassic Park* all *rawr* and shit. Talk! Tell that woman you love her or all of this will be for nothing, and that'll be annoying because I had chel plans today."

"What's shell?" Hollis whispers as if they can hear us.

"*Chel*," I correct. "Hockey slang for the NHL video game. Say it fast and it sounds like chel."

She screws her nose up. "Uh, but he plays *in* the NHL—why not just do the real thing?"

"Who knows." I shrug. "Boys are weird."

Miller and Smith continue to argue, and it's becoming more and more apparent that neither of them is aware the camera is on.

"Yeah, buddy!" I hear someone shout, and it sounds a lot like Rhodes. "We have shit to do today! Let's get a move on."

"Pitter-fucking-patter," another voice—definitely belonging to Collin—adds.

"Hollis can only distract her for so long," Lowell chimes in. "And I want to snuggle my baby."

"See? Shit to do. Just be like, 'Hey, hot tits,'" Miller says, imitating a deep voice.

Smith's growl is *very* audible. "Miller…"

"Fine. 'Hey, hot ass, I retired from the NHL for you, and I love you and shit. Want to get out of here and bone?' And that's it. That's all you have to say."

I gasp.

Smith…retired?

308

I don't think. I just run.

I run right out into the rink.

When I reach the top of the stairs, I pause, and there he is, standing center ice, scowling at Miller, who is trying to shove the camera back in his face.

"Smith!"

He looks up, and his whole face transforms. Gone is the scowl, replaced by pure love and adoration.

And it's all for me.

"You retired?" I shout.

He nods. "This morning! The press release goes out tomorrow, but I thought—"

"Hey, can you come down here? I don't think the camera is picking up the audio very well," Miller yells, pointing it at me.

And I start running all over again. Down the stairs, dodging through seats, not stopping until I'm sliding onto the ice, looking like a newborn calf slipping around.

Smith is there to catch me before I can fall.

"Thank fuck," he mutters, wrapping me in his arms and crushing his mouth to mine.

Just like that, everything is right in my world again. I sag against him, relishing the way his body feels against mine, the way we fit so perfectly together. It makes me want to cry.

"Oh, thank fuck!" Rhodes calls. "I'm out of here."

I faintly hear the other guys mutter something similar.

"Please don't fire me!" Blake says from somewhere,

his voice getting smaller and smaller as he likely follows everyone else down the tunnel. "I need this job, and Nate can't strip, remember?"

He laughs nervously, and then we're alone.

Only then does Smith pull his mouth from mine. He looks down at me, his tawny-brown eyes that I love so much bouncing between my green ones, a smile tugging at his lips.

"Hi," he says quietly.

"Hi. You really retired?"

"I really did."

"But...why?"

"Because I choose you."

My breathing stutters at his words. "You choose me?"

He nods. "I've had my chance to chase my dream of playing the greatest game in the world. Now, it's your turn to chase yours."

"But—"

He shakes his head, cutting me off. "No. No buts, not even hockey ones—not about this. I've thought about it a lot, and this is what I want. *You're* what I want."

I sigh, and he laughs just before pressing his lips to my mouth again.

He runs his nose along mine when he pulls away. "I love you, you know?"

"I know."

"Like really, *really* love you. I have for a while, I think. Hell, maybe I even fell that first weekend."

"I think that's a real possibility. I'm very loveable, and I give great head."

He chuckles. "That so?"

"Yes." I give him a quick peck on the lips. "You're not with the Comets anymore... Which means we wouldn't be breaking any rules..."

"I'm not *playing* for the Comets anymore," he clarifies, "but I do plan to keep working with the team unofficially."

My heart sinks. "What...what does that mean for us?"

"Not a damn thing. We're good."

"We are?"

He nods. "Yes. I read that handbook forward and back. I'm not part of the organization, so we can do whatever we want."

I let out a relieved sigh. "That's the greatest thing I've ever heard."

"Yeah? Did you miss the part where I said I love you?"

"Possibly. You're going to have to repeat it a few more times."

"I."

Kiss.

"Love."

Kiss.

"You."

Kiss.

"So damn much, Emilia. I didn't realize I was

missing something so important in my life until you. I didn't realize that I could feel this way about anything other than hockey until you. I didn't realize that I wanted more out of life than hockey until you. But I do. I want it all. A future."

I sigh. "I haven't been the same since our first weekend together. I've been trying to deny it and pretend and bury myself in work, but I should have known it was useless. I had no chance at fighting it. Not really. Not when you make me feel the way you do. I love you, and I want that future too. Everything. All of it."

"Yeah?" he asks.

I nod. "Yeah."

Our mouths crash together again, and we don't let up, not until I'm shivering in Smith's arms, the cold of the ice seeping into my bones.

"Come on. Let's get you out of here," he says, leading me toward the exit.

"What exactly were the guys here for?"

Smith shrugs. "No clue. That was all Miller."

"To take your sorry ass to the bar if she decided she didn't want your saggy old man balls!" Miller calls out, and we turn to find him sitting on the bench, still recording.

"Miller…" Smith growls, turning toward him.

"Oh shit!" The kid takes off running as fast as he can on skates, dashing down the tunnel for safety.

Smith shakes his head, helping me off the ice. "He's a fucking menace."

"But you love him."

He pulls me right back into his arms, and I sink into him.

This is where I belong.

"I love *you*," he whispers against my lips.

"And I love you more...*Owen*."

EPILOGUE

I've been officially retired for a few months now but looking out at the group of people smiling at me makes it feel real for the first time.

I am done with hockey.

Well, not *done* done. I'm still working for the Comets. I signed on the dotted line just a month ago and am now officially an assistant video coach for the team I love.

It's weird, but I also can't deny the weight lifted off my shoulders. It's freeing in a way I wasn't expecting. I miss it, but I also don't. Not the way I expected to miss it.

That could be because I'm still involved in the game, but it could also be because my days are full of everything I didn't realize I was missing. Spending time with Emilia and being able to be open with our relationship was worth giving up the game. Being with her gives me a better high than being on the ice ever did.

Emilia's arm slips around my waist, bringing me back to the here and now. I tug her closer, relishing the way she fits so perfectly tucked under my arm.

"You good?" she whispers from beside me.

I peer down at the redheaded beauty grinning up at me. I know her well enough to know that the smile she's sending my way is full of worry and uncertainty.

Probably because all our friends are standing in front of us with a sign that reads *Happy Retirement, Old Man.* I thought we were coming here for a quiet game night. Hell, I even have a puzzle tucked under my arm right now.

Apparently, I've been misled. This isn't a game night. This is a surprise retirement party. Lowell's house is decorated with streamers and balloons, and a few tables are set up with different kinds of snacks. There are members of the coaching staff scattered around, and even Blake is here with his husband.

Everyone stares at me with a grin, eagerly waiting for my reaction.

It's hard to give one, especially with the emotion in my throat. This is the exact reason I didn't want to make a big deal about my retirement and do it after the season ended. It's tough handling the emotions that come with it internally, never mind in front of a crowd. Just standing here, I can feel the tightness worsening and the sting of tears threatening to form.

Emilia tightens her hold on me because of course *she* knows why I can't talk right now.

"Dude, can you react or something? This is getting awkward as fuck."

"Shut up, Miller!" Rhodes yells at him, smacking the back of his head.

Everyone laughs, and the tension in the room is broken.

"Thanks, guys," I say, blinking a few times, hoping nobody notices I'm about two seconds away from crying. "I appreciate it."

"Speech!" someone hollers from the back, and it sounds suspiciously like Collin is just deepening his voice.

Emilia gives me another encouraging squeeze.

I clear my throat. "I don't have anything prepared because, clearly, this wasn't what I thought tonight was going to be." I shake the puzzle box as proof.

"What kind of old man brings a puzzle to game night?" Miller says, and it earns him another slap, this time from Lowell.

"Hockey has been my life for...well, all my life. It's been everything to me for a long time, and spending these last few years with everyone in this room has made me love the game even harder...and that's with having Miller on the team."

"Aww," the guy in question says, placing his hand over his heart.

"Because of that, deciding to hang up my skates wasn't an easy one. It was easily the hardest thing I ever had to decide. But..." I peek down at Emilia, who is watching me with tears glistening in her eyes. "While I might love the game of hockey and you guys too, there's someone else I love more. And I'd choose her every time."

A single tear slips down Emilia's cheek, and I wish like fuck we weren't in a room full of people right now because I want so badly to haul her into my arms, kiss away the tears, then strip her bare.

"Fucking hell, Emilia, if you don't kiss him after that, I will."

Lowell groans at Miller's outburst. "Can we duct tape his mouth and handcuff him in the spare bedroom until he promises to act right?"

"I just really want to know why you have duct tape and handcuffs on standby," Miller says.

"You know, as much as I hate agreeing with him, I'm curious too," Collin agrees.

"Got to be a kinky sex thing for sure," Rhodes adds.

"Like you have room to talk about kinky sex things," Ryan mutters to her husband.

Everyone turns their attention to Rhodes, whose cheeks are growing redder by the second. They all start talking over each other, trying to guess each other's kinks.

I ignore them, grabbing Emilia's hand and tugging her away from their idiocy. I sit the puzzle box on the table in the entryway and draw her into my arms.

She grins up at me. "You surprised?"

"Very much so."

"You're not mad, are you? I know you're not super fond of crowds, but they really wanted to do something for you."

"Not mad," I assure her. "Grateful."

"Yeah?"

"Yeah." I nod. "And mildly annoyed that there are so many people around because I really, *really* want to show you just how grateful I am." I press against her tighter, and there's no way she doesn't feel my growing cock. "You think they'll notice if we sneak off for a few minutes?"

"Even if they do, I don't care."

I grab her hand to drag her down the hall toward the bedrooms.

We don't make it two feet before the front door flies open.

"Oh my gosh!" Scout says, scurrying over the threshold with a stack of boxes in her hand. "I am *so* sorry I'm late, Emilia. There was a whole thing with traffic, and the security guard wouldn't let me in the neighborhood. But I brought donuts!"

"Don't worry about it. We're glad you made it," Emilia says, stepping toward her.

She's brushed aside by Miller, who comes out of nowhere, reaching for the boxes.

"I can take those for you," he says to Scout, who is staring at him with wide eyes.

"T-Thanks," she says quietly.

"Sure thing. I'm Grady, by the way. It's nice to meet you."

I'm about to tell Miller he's an idiot for not recognizing Scout from the donut truck, but I don't have the chance to. Scout pulls the boxes closer to her chest and brushes past him like he never spoke at all, clearly—and rightfully—annoyed with him.

"What'd I say?" Miller mutters, following closely behind her.

Emilia laughs, and I shake my head at the idiot, watching as he trails after Scout looking like someone punched him in the gut.

"He's going to have some fun digging himself out of that hole he just created," Emilia says.

"I don't think fun is the right word, but I can't wait to watch either way. But first…" I grab her hand, heading for the bedrooms for the second time.

This time we make it three steps before we're stopped.

"Hey, Smith! Come tell Greer about that insane goal you scored my first season," Lowell shouts, waving us over.

I groan because all I really want right now is to sneak away with Emilia.

She laughs, understanding my frustration.

"Rain check on showing me how grateful you are?"

"*Checks*," I growl, wrapping my arms around her and settling for a chaste kiss. "Plural."

"Ooh. I like the way you think, Mr. Smith."

"Owen. I'm not one of your players anymore, you know."

"I know, and I love it."

"Yeah?" I kiss the tip of her nose. "Well, I love *you*."

She sighs, falling against me. "And I love you, *Owen*."

And I know at this moment that I'll choose her for the rest of my life.

**

Thank you for reading **SIN BIN**!
I hope you enjoyed Emilia & Smith.

Want more Carolina Comets?
SCORING CHANCE (Miller's book) is up next!

Want more Emilia & Smith?
Sign up for my newsletter for a bonus scene!

Looking for more Comets but not sure where to start?
PUCK SHY is available now!

OTHER TITLES BY TEAGAN HUNTER

Cheesy on the Eyes

TEXTING SERIES

Let's Get Textual

I Wanna Text You Up

Can't Text This

Text Me Baby One More Time

INTERCONNECTED STANDALONES

We Are the Stars

If You Say So

HERE'S TO SERIES

Here's to Tomorrow

Here's to Yesterday

Here's to Forever: A Novella

Here's to Now

Want to be part of a fun reader group, gain access to exclusive content and giveaways, and get to know me more?

Join Teagan's Tidbits on Facebook!

Want to stay on top of my new releases?

Sign up for my newsletter!

ACKNOWLEDGMENTS

This book wouldn't be possible without the support of these amazing people:

The Marine (my husband)

Laurie (the world's best PA & friend)

My Editing Team - Caitlin, Julia, & Julie

#soulmate Kristann

sMother

Miranda & Lindsey (my sisters)

All of the Bloggers, Bookstagrammers, and BookTokers who have taken a chance on me.

My Tidbits, the best Facebook group around

And **YOU**.

With love and unwavering gratitude,

Teagan

TEAGAN HUNTER is a Missouri-raised gal, but currently lives in South Carolina with her Marine veteran husband, where she spends her days begging him for a cat. She survives off of coffee, pizza, and sarcasm. When not writing, you can find her binge-watching *Supernatural* or *One Tree Hill*. She enjoys cold weather, buys more paperbacks than she'll ever read, and never says no to brownies.

www.teaganhunterwrites.com

CPSIA information can be obtained
at www.ICGtesting.com
Printed in the USA
BVHW031724070323
659898BV00018B/209

9 781737 548195